Our Troubles

To my wife, Isolde, for her support
and encouragement over the years

Our
Troubles

by

Anthony CANAVAN

PHÆTON
PUBLISHING LTD.
—— Dublin ——

Our Troubles

FIRST PUBLISHED IN IRELAND & U.K. 2024
by Phaeton Publishing Limited, Dublin

Copyright © Anthony CANAVAN, 2024

Anthony CANAVAN has asserted his right
to be identified as the author of this work

Cover & book design copyright ©
O'Dwyer & Jones Design Partnership, 2024

*British Library Cataloguing In Publication
Data : a catalogue record for this book
is available from the British Library*

ISBN: 978-1-908420-33-6 PAPERBACK
ISBN: 978-1-908420-34-3 HARDBACK

Inset front cover photograph of barricade in
Belfast taken by Séamas Ó CATHÁIN 1969

Contents

BELFAST
During the Troubles

BASED ON BELFAST CONSTITUENCY & WARD MAP OF 1995

Foreword

by Tim McGarry

IN THE INTERESTS OF transparency and objectivity I should tell the reader that I know Tony Canavan and have been an acquaintance of his for many years. On the other hand I don't know Tony well enough, nor indeed do I like him sufficiently, that I could be induced to lie on his behalf. Furthermore, I regret to say, that whilst he asked me to write this introductory piece, absolutely no money has been proffered or changed hands. Therefore I can, with a completely clear conscience, confirm that this foreword is entirely impartial and unprejudiced.

Tony is a highly experienced and distinguished historian, researcher and editor. He has appeared on the excellent BBC Radio Ulster history series *The Long and the Short of it* – a highlight of his career. But can he write? Yes, thankfully.

Our Troubles is a collection of charming, deceptively disarming, and moving stories set during the Northern Ireland Troubles which ran from the late 1960s and ended, formally, with the Good Friday Agreement of 1998.

Our protagonist is called Finn, a Catholic from a nationalist background who lives in North Belfast. *Our Troubles* follows him from his first day at grammar school to his going to university.

If you were to look at contemporary photographs of Tony and me you would undoubtedly come to the obvious conclusion that he is considerably older than me. Alas, this is not the case. He is my senior but only by a few years. We are near contemporaries. This means that the stories, the events, the people, and the places that appear in *Our Troubles* are completely familiar to me.

I am from North Belfast, an area which experienced the

worst of the conflict and suffered a disproportionate number of casualties.

Each of Tony's stories felt entirely authentic to me. I know the streets he is talking about, I wore the uniform of St Malachy's College for seven years myself, and I remember the soldiers and the paramilitaries and the riots. (But just to reiterate – I am younger than him.)

There have been countless books written about the Troubles by historians and fiction writers. What is often missed, and what Tony's book perfectly brings to life, is the ordinary lives of people living through extraordinary times. The stories of people with no paramilitary or political connections are often overlooked. Tony tells those stories – the tales of the daily struggles, the absurdities, and the attempts by people to survive and live life as best they can.

Through his wonderfully evocative stories, Tony has successfully brought to life that strange, awful, confusing, and fractious time in the history of Northern Ireland. Through the eyes of Finn, he captures the normal abnormalities of growing up in North Belfast. From the quirks of school uniforms, being stopped by the army, how streets became segregated, to the ever-present sectarianism and ever-looming violence, *Our Troubles* will entertain whilst simultaneously telling you why Northern Ireland has come to be the place it is in 2024.

Tony's stories will make you smile, make you reminisce and, if you are younger in years, make you think 'what the feck were those people on back then?!!!'

Our Troubles is poignant, funny, and sad. It brought me back to my childhood, a time I look back on with fondness but to which I never want to return.

Tim McGarry 2024

Tim McGarry, comedian, actor, and writer, is a member of the comedy group *The Hole in the Wall Gang*, and writer of (and actor in) the satirical BBC television comedy series *Give My Head Peace*.

Introduction

I WAS BORN AND BRED (as we say in my home town) in North Belfast, an area that saw some of the worst of the communal conflict known as the Troubles. Approximately 16% of all the fatalities of the Troubles occurred there.

Although the street I grew up in and those around it were mixed, that is both Catholic and Protestant families lived there, I was introduced to sectarianism at a young age. One of my earliest encounters occurred when I was five or six: a trio of older boys punched and kicked me for being 'a Fenian bastard.' This happened just a couple of streets from where I lived and I was ignorant of what it meant to be a Fenian or a bastard. My parents, hard-working people from the Falls Road, had tried to shelter their children from sectarianism, but its presence was all pervasive. I was not very old when I began to understand the significance of Orange bands marching past our street all through summer. Knowing that Catholics lived there, the parade would stop and play particularly loudly to the rhythm of the ferocious Lambeg drum.

When the Troubles did break out in 1968, our street remained mixed and the residents did their best to keep the strife at bay. However, this did not last long and soon we were exposed to events as much as anyone, more than many. Rumours and unattributed instructions began to sow discontent among locals. Most of these seemed to emanate from the Loyalist side: there were rumours that they intended to burn out the Catholic inhabitants of the mixed streets and instructions that Protestants should move out. These were soon followed by actual violence: from low level stuff, like myself or schoolmates being beaten up by Loyalist youths, to the murder of Catholics in their own homes. As well as this, there was the RUC and the British Army presence which did not make life easier. The IRA were not a noticeable presence in this area, even after the streets became almost totally Catholic. On a couple of occasions in the early 1970s, an IRA man, usually from Ardoyne, fended off a Loyalist mob by firing a few shots in their direction. Apart from that, the IRA was more talked about than seen.

Most people just tried to get on with their lives. Those that had jobs went to them each day, not knowing if they would come home in one piece. Women, as the times dictated, did their best to keep the home clean and their family happy, although many of them (like my mother and some of my aunts) had part-time jobs also. No house in our street or the neighbouring ones was actually burned down, although windows were stoned if within range of the notorious 'River Streets,' a Loyalist enclave near the Oldpark Road. Funerals were a common feature of our existence as people were killed – usually shot, but sometimes the victims of bombs. When the Shankill Butchers were active, the area between Cliftonville Road and Oldpark Road was part of their hunting ground, making going out on foot after dark a foreboding prospect.

I was personally affected by the loss of two uncles, murdered by Loyalists, and more indirectly when three of my aunts and their families were forced out of their homes in Annalee Street by a Loyalist mob while the British Army looked on. Also two of my cousins spent time in Long Kesh for their involvement with the IRA. In my wider circle, friends that I had been to school with were killed in the Troubles or served time in prison. Some people just went away and were never heard of again.

The stories in this collection mostly have the same theme, which is that they are all informed by my experiences growing up in North Belfast during the Troubles. I have always felt that the lives of ordinary Catholics during those years have largely been left out of the narrative of the Troubles. All the events related in these stories are inspired by things that actually happened to my family, friends, or myself. There is a central character, Finn, around whom most of the stories are told. Like all the characters in the collection, he is not based on one individual but inspired by a number of people.

Anthony CANAVAN

Our Troubles

MASSERENE STREET, FALLS ROAD AREA, BELFAST, 1967

Neighbours

E VEN NOW over fifty years later, Finn could not see a Union Jack flying without thinking of that day – the day the Troubles began for him. He was only eleven at the time and the attacks on civil rights marchers, riots, and police baton charges were things to watch on TV. He and his friends knew of course what was happening and occasionally they could see plumes of smoke rising above the rooftops far off and even smell burning, an acrid smell that hung in the air for hours. His father and mother spoke of the trouble on the streets, and his mother thanked God that they no longer lived on the Falls Road where things were bad.

Finn's family, the Conlyns, lived in a mixed district in North Belfast. Finn's street consisted mainly of newly arrived Catholic families, most of whom had moved from West Belfast like Finn's parents. There were no Protestant children in the street. What Protestants there were, were aging couples in retirement or close to it. His own parents had met and married on the Falls Road, where they had been born and bred. They both came from working-class families in that Catholic stronghold. Finn knew the houses where they had grown up because every Saturday they took the NO. 77 bus back to the Falls Road to visit his grannies. They still lived in the small terraced houses with just two rooms upstairs and down. There they had raised their families, sometimes two or three to a bed. Finn's father – his name was Patrick but everyone called him Pat – had a good job as a roofer, working for his uncle. The work was hard and the days could be long but it paid well enough. His mother worked too, part-time as a stitcher in a small factory in the city centre. Together they saved their money to buy a better house than they had grown up in, and getting away from the Falls was the best option.

They were each the first of their families to leave West Belfast and move into a bigger house with a small front garden as well as a yard at the back. It meant a big deal then and even years afterwards.

Finn had been born and raised in that house. He played in the surrounding streets with his friends who all went to his school. They were all Catholics together and their parents all came from similar backgrounds except the two to three whose families had moved here from the country – and anywhere outside Belfast was the country. Further along were a few other mixed streets of Catholic and Protestant families. By some twist of demographics, there were Protestant kids in these streets but they went to their own school and some invisible barrier kept them apart from the Catholic children except for the odd occasion when a fight would break out. Beyond that were the River Streets, called after Irish rivers, and no Catholic ever went there.

The only Protestants that Finn knew to speak to were the Clarks. They lived a few doors down from the Conlyns. They were an elderly couple and their two sons, young men in their twenties, lived at home. The whole family was held in some regard in the street, especially by the Catholics, because they belonged to a small Protestant church which was associated with good works and a moral lifestyle. They did not drink or go out to dances or even the cinema. None of the Clarks had joined the Orange Order and they weren't involved in politics. They were friendly with the Conlyns. One of the sons was in the Territorial Army and he would give surplus gear to Finn's father to wear while working on the roofs as they were more hard wearing than ordinary working clothes.

When the trouble in the city got closer to their own district, Pat and the other men of the mixed streets formed a committee to keep the peace and watch out for troublemakers. Every night both Catholic and Protestant neighbours, including the Clark boys, formed patrols to walk the area and keep an eye on things. They wore white armbands and carried an odd assortment of arms: walking sticks, pickaxe handles, one of them even carried a shillelagh he'd picked up on a holiday in

Killarney. They patrolled in twos and threes, asking strangers what they were doing here, and taking note of strange cars. However, the only excitement they had was one night when a whistle sounded an alarm and they rushed to the bottom of the street to see two of the patrol confronting men in a strange car. There was a crash of bottles as a milk crate loaded with petrol bombs fell to the ground and the car sped off. It went in the direction of the River Streets, the Protestant enclave. This incident sent ripples through the committee. Who were these men out to get? Not the Protestant families. Who you could trust if it came down to it... ?

Every evening after they'd had their dinner, Finn watched his father put on his jacket with the white armband and take his pick-axe handle before he went out on patrol. His mother might give him a flask of tea and a bag of sandwiches if he was going to be out all night. Finn looked on this with some excitement. It was like his father was a soldier or some kind of hero going out to defend his people. Looking back, he now realised that to his father also it was exciting, a break from the humdrum of everyday life. His father was generally an easygoing man who was popular with the people in their street. This put him at the centre of the vigilante committee, an unofficial leader.

As summer wore on, the threats to the area heightened. It was said that the Orangemen were coming to burn the Catholics out. The UVF had threatened to shoot people down in the street and the RUC from the nearest barracks had made it clear that they would not intervene if the mixed streets were attacked. These were just rumours but then something definite happened. Someone claimed to have certain knowledge that the UVF was coming in strength soon to burn out the Catholics in the mixed streets. An order had gone out that Protestant houses were to hang out the Union Jack so that they would not be attacked.

Some people dismissed this as just another rumour; others believed it. But no one thought that their Protestant neighbours would hang out flags. Finn's father flatly rejected the idea when another Catholic said it would happen, but the man was insistent. The next day a Union Jack flew from outside the Clarks' house. Almost every house in Finn's street had a bracket and socket to take a flagpole. It had not meant much to him as a child. His father took the family away every July, south of the border where they would not have to endure the Union Jacks and Orange marches. Now these sockets carried new significance, and Finn realised that all these houses must have flown the Union Jack, the British flag, every July. All that is except the houses which the Catholics had moved into. Now the solitary flag on Clarks' house flew like a warning.

The Clarks' flag was discussed at the vigilante committee meeting that night. The meeting was not well attended. A few of the Catholic men stayed away and most of the Protestants. Those that did come said they would stand by their Catholic neighbours and maintain the peace. The Clarks were not at the meeting. When it ended, the Catholic men gathered outside to discuss what to do if the UVF did attack the street as they now believed they would. Defend the street? Leave? Ask their Protestant neighbours for help? Could they trust their Protestant neighbours? What about the Clarks? They broke up in indecision and confusion but the last words spoken were by Finn's father, 'If I'm burned out of my house then I'll make sure that a house flying the Union Jack goes up in smoke too. If it's the last thing I do.'

The next evening, just as they were finishing dinner, the doorbell rang and Pat went to see who it was. Old Mr Clark, all Protestant respectability in his suit and tie, stood there with his two sons. Finn slipped into the hall and retreated up the stairs, far enough not to be seen from the hall door but close enough to hear what was going on. Mr Clark was a large fat man and his sons were tall and well built. They all towered over Finn's father. Pat was not a tall man but in all Finn's life he had never seen him show fear or back down before any threat. Finn watched with a mixture of excitement and apprehension.

'I hear you have a problem with us flying our flag,' began Mr Clark.

'It's the reason you're flying it that I've a problem with,' Pat replied.

'I don't know what you mean. We fly that flag every year. We're loyal citizens.'

'You fly it every July. It's still only June now. So why are you flying it?'

'There's no law against it, Mr Conlyn.' This from one of the sons.

'You haven't answered my question. Why fly it in June?'

'We just decided to put it up early. What's the problem in that?'

'You know the problem. Are you seriously telling me it's just coincidence that the day after we get word that the UVF plans to burn out this street, and asks Protestant families to put out the Union Jack, that you hang out yours?'

From his perch on the stairs, Finn could feel the tension in the air. The Clarks had always been friendly, if not exactly warm, but here they were all bristling with anger and giving off hostile vibes. All of which was met in equal measure by his father. The Clarks stayed silent in reply to his father's question; they just stared at him. Finn thought it was just like a Western when men faced off against each other, waiting to see who would draw first. Finn felt afraid. The Clarks were scary now and there was three of them against his father. He thought that his dad was standing up to them like Joe Starrett against the bullying cattlemen, but his dad didn't have Shane to back him up. The silence seemed to last for minutes and the tension was palpable.

Then finally Mr Clark spoke, 'If that's the way you feel about it …'

'We're not ashamed of being Protestants,' one of the sons said aggressively.

'I thought we were neighbours,' Pat said, 'I've fixed your roof and not asked for a penny. We've lent each other tools. Look how many times last winter I gave you a push to start your car. We've lived together side by side for years. I thought we were neighbours.'

'Ach, you know how it is. These times. You know as well as we do what's going on.'

'Do you realise what this house means to us? My wife and I stayed a year in her sister's spare room saving every penny to put down a deposit on a decent house. I grew up sharing a room with three brothers. I wanted my children to enjoy a bedroom of their own. We scrimp, we save, we put every spare penny into paying off the mortgage. This is our home. We've nowhere else to go.'

'We've got to put ourselves first. You'd do the same,' said one of the Clark boys.

'No, I wouldn't,' Pat replied. 'If we had stuck together. If no one had put up a flag, they wouldn't dare come into this street. Now your flag's an invitation.'

'Don't be like that, Mr Conlyn,' Mr Clark pleaded, 'My wife's worried sick. I had to put the flag out.'

'Don't hide behind your wife,' Finn's dad said.

Finn had to sneak a look out to be sure it really was him, for suddenly he sounded like Shane. His voice was hard and provocative. It was like he was telling Mr Clark to go for his gun.

Another silence followed.

Again Mr Clark spoke first, 'Well we've put the flag out and that's it. We're not taking it down now.'

Still in his hard Shane-like voice, his father replied, 'I'm telling you now. If this house gets burned down because you put out that butcher's apron, then I'll see to it that your house is next.'

The three taller men took a step away from the door. The resolve in Pat's voice had knocked them back like a physical force.

'If that's the way you feel about it, Conlyn, there's nothing more we can do,' said Mr Clark.

'I'm not putting up with this,' interrupted the older son. 'We've a right to do what we want. I'm not going to be bullied by a Fenian. The time has come to make a choice and we're Protestants. The flag stays!'

'Quiet, son, don't start that now.'

Father and sons faced each other before Mr Clark turned to Pat saying, 'Sorry, the flag has to stay.'

'It's your choice,' said Finn's father but the others had already turned to leave.

The flag stayed up that day but was down by the next morning. No one saw them take the flag down and no other flags went up. The Loyalists did not come to burn out the Catholic families, not then at any rate. In July the Conlyn family went south of the Border for their annual holiday. Not as usual since Mr Conlyn, like the other Catholic fathers and husbands, stayed behind to stand guard over their house just in case the UVF did come to burn them out. When Finn came back to Belfast at the end of July there was a FOR-SALE sign on the Clarks' house. He never saw the Clarks again. They had moved out to some other part of the city before the house was sold. When it was, another Catholic family bought it.

The attempt to keep trouble away from the mixed streets had failed. For Finn, that was when the Troubles became real. How easily someone could be frightened into betraying his neighbour and how that neighbour would hit back. The incident over the flag was only the beginning; a small thing compared to the murderous attacks on the mixed streets that would happen in the following years. Yet for Finn the stand-off over the flag was the most vivid memory.

Loss of Innocence

AUNT MAGGIE was not Finn's favourite, though she thought she was. She thought that she was everyone's favourite aunt. His mother's younger sister, she had what people euphemistically called a larger-than-life personality. For as long as he could remember, Finn dreaded her visits. She would arrive in the house generating noise, bluster, and a cloud of perfume. She insisted on talking to Finn, calling him out of his bedroom where he sought sanctuary, demanding to see his latest toys and inquiring about how he was doing at school. She was in no way nasty but her benevolence was overbearing. Her misplaced advice and show of concern over the slightest thing was disconcerting. She often threatened to turn up at Finn's school and give his teacher a piece of her mind for giving him too much homework or a low grade in his tests. But she never did, much to Finn's relief. Maggie had been a performer on the stage in her childhood. She could sing and dance and often won talent competitions, not just in Belfast but throughout Ireland. For a brief period she was something of a celebrity on the Falls Road in the 1940s, regularly appearing at shows in parish halls or doing a turn in social clubs.

All that stopped when she had to leave school at fourteen and get a job. She still missed the glamour of show business and always had airs and graces, as Finn's mother put it. Aunt Maggie always spoke in a very proper way. She avoided slang words and never ever used swear words, in contrast to Finn's aunts on the other side who were sharp-witted women not above the occasional Anglo-Saxon expletive. Maggie's outgoing personality made her a success in the department store where she eventually settled after a couple of other jobs didn't work out. It was a big store on Royal Avenue, owned by a prominent Unionist family. Beth, Finn's mother, used to joke that she only got the job because her name, Margaret Stewart, sounded Protestant, but Maggie was convinced that she got the job on merit and that there was not a bigoted bone in her employer's body. Her willingness to engage with customers and to offer sincere advice about the clothes that suited them, made her a hit in the ladies department, and her fellow workers thought she was a hoot. That was something else she missed, once she had to give up work when she married.

Peter, her husband, hadn't wanted Maggie to quit work when they married, but she had notions of being the perfect housewife in the perfect wee house. It was the only house Finn knew where a cup of tea and a bun involved so much fuss. Aunt Maggie insisted on lace doilies, place mats, and even sugar tongs. Not that he was in her house much. It was not the kind of house where a child could feel at ease. Even Finn's mam could never relax in her sister's house. Everything was prim and proper and she was always afraid of breaking some decorative knickknack or other. Sometimes, if she had no other choice, Finn's mother would ask Aunt Maggie to babysit Finn and his brother and sister while she went off shopping on a Saturday afternoon. Finn was prepared to put up with all the fuss because Aunt Maggie had a television set long before his parents could afford one, and he had to admit that she was a good singer. Every visit included switching off the television while she did a reprise of her stage show. Finn's younger sister, Helen, loved this and began to have her own dreams of becoming a music star.

Sometimes Peter was there too and he helped dilute Maggie's presence. Peter was known as The Quiet Man to his in-laws. They joked that with Maggie around he never got the chance to speak, In fact, when Maggie wasn't around, Peter was a different man. Maggie wasn't one for what she called rowdiness, so she would often leave family gatherings, weddings or birthday parties, early, warning her brothers not to lead Peter astray. Once Maggie was out of the way, Peter let himself go. He could drink with the best of them and told hilarious lewd jokes. He revealed that he could play the guitar and sing a bit. This didn't happen very often as most of the time he was happy to follow his wife's lead and go home early with her. Finn didn't see this side of his uncle and thought him hen-pecked, a term he had recently picked up from television.

All might have proceeded along like this, with Finn showing a tolerance for Aunt Maggie's eccentricities that only a knowing child can show an adult, if it hadn't been for the Troubles. As with everything else, Aunt Maggie had to share her opinion of what was happening with everyone she knew, including Finn. She had not approved of the Civil Rights Movement as she said it would only lead to trouble and felt vindicated when the first riots started. In her view it was troublemakers, rowdies she called them, who were out to cause bother. A load of layabouts who would be better off getting a job, was her opinion.

By now twelve years old, Finn was just becoming aware of the world around him. Even as a young boy, he'd been beaten up by older Protestant kids for being a Fenian, so he knew there was hostility between Catholic and Protestant. Growing up in such circumstances, he had just accepted this as the natural order of things, but he was beginning to realise that there were bigger issues at stake, and that Catholic and Protestant were just shorthand for political beliefs and identities. He now consciously thought of himself as Irish and understood what the adults said when they talked about wanting a united Ireland.

Aunt Maggie didn't want a united Ireland; she couldn't see the point. Her and Peter lived in a nice house in a nice lower-middle-class part of North Belfast, and she got on with her Protestant neighbours. Her politics were that the Catholics should just be more serious, work hard, and get on with their neighbours, just like her and Peter. Even at his age, Finn couldn't understand how anyone could be so blind to what was going on around them. His attitude led to arguments with Aunt Maggie, when he challenged her on what she was saying about the rioters and the decency of the RUC, and so on. She reacted with outraged indignation and, rather than answer him, she took it out on his mother and chastised her for not bringing her children up properly. After he had argued with Aunt Maggie a couple of times, Finn's mum would plead with him not to agitate his aunt and eventually he let her speak without contradiction.

Part of Aunt Maggie's 'airs and graces' was an admiration for all things English, including their royal family. She often spoke of moving to England, saying that she kept asking Peter to apply for a job there. No one took this talk very seriously, even though everyone knew someone who had emigrated to Britain or further afield. Maggie was different in that her motives for leaving weren't purely economic. 'She says more than her prayers,' was Finn's mother's opinion if anyone asked if Maggie was serious about going across the water. So it came as a surprise one day when she announced on a visit to her sister that Peter had been offered a job in Leicester with an insurance company and that, within a month, they'd both be heading across the water. Beth didn't know what to say beyond, 'Are you sure it's what you want?'

'The way this place is going,' replied Aunt Maggie, 'with fighting on the streets and people being burned out of their homes, I wouldn't want to stay here. And, sure, it's only getting worse. With the IRA starting up again, nobody will be safe in their beds.'

Beth did try to persuade her sister to stay but it was no use, Maggie had her mind made up. Peter was going to a great job in an insurance company and they'd found a house and all for them.

The plan was that Peter would go over to Leicester a week before Maggie, to settle into the new job and get what was needed for the house. Then Maggie would take the ferry and follow him. The day before he was due to leave, Peter drove down to the Falls Road to visit his mother. He wanted to see her on his own and say goodbye to her properly before he caught the ferry the next day, Saturday. This was not the same neighbourhood where he had grown up. He had been born and bred in Scotch Street in the Loney, but the whole area had been demolished and the Divis Flats complex built where once there had been streets of wee terraced houses. All the families from the Loney had been forced to move into these flats. He had moved out by then but he still had nostalgia for the old place. His mother, a widow, now lived in a small modern house in Albert Street. After leaving his mother, Peter decided that since he was in the neighbourhood, he would call in to an old friend from his Scotch Street days that he still kept in touch with, to say goodbye. Martin persuaded Peter to go out for one last drink and he was happy enough to do that. After all, this would probably be his last chance to share a drink with his old friends. Who knew what England would be like?

Peter had no idea that all hell was about to break loose. That afternoon a large force of RUC men and members of the Royal Scots Regiment entered the Lower Falls to carry out a weapons search. They began with a raid on a house on Balkan Street, a good bit up the road from where Peter and his mates were drinking, oblivious to what was happening. A column of armoured vehicles sealed off the street. The soldiers and RUC men spent about forty-five minutes searching the house before finding some guns and a stash of ammunition. This was more than enough time for a protest to be organised. As the military column was endeavouring to leave the street, a gang of local lads attacked the soldiers with stones and petrol bombs. As was now becoming familiar, the soldiers responded with CS gas. A running battle ensued as stones and bottles were met with CS gas rounds. From somewhere, armed IRA men appeared and opened fire on the soldiers. More soldiers were called to the scene and soon open warfare broke out in the narrow streets running off the Falls Road.

Peter spent more time in the pub than he had intended, but he had got caught up in their nostalgic talk of their childhood days and it was hard to say no to the pints he was offered. He came out onto the Falls Road and smelled the CS gas drifting down from where the trouble was and heard sirens getting closer. His eyes began to sting and he realised that it was time to get out of there. He proceeded as quickly as he could down the Falls to Albert Street where he had parked the car. Jeeps and lorries full of soldiers raced passed him. The presence of television crews gave an unreal feeling to it all, like he was the extra in the shooting of a film. Pressing on, Peter arrived at the top of Albert Street just as two army lorries and an armoured car parked across it, preventing entry or exit.

Peter just wanted to get his car and go home. He had nothing to do with this trouble. The smell of smoke and CS gas, combined with the sound of gunfire was pushing him towards panic. Gingerly he approached the gap between the two lorries where a soldier in battledress was on guard. As Peter approached, he raised his rifle and pointed it at him.

'What'd you want?' he said in a thick Scottish accent.

'I just want to go down there and get my car.'

'Nobody goes in or out.'

'You don't understand. I don't belong here. I'm just visiting and want to go home.'

'Listen, pal,' said the soldier aggressively, 'No one gets in or out. Got it?'

Peter tried again to explain that he just wanted his car and then he'd be on his way. Again the soldier told him it was no go. Perhaps Peter shouldn't have had that last pint. He was getting angry and indignant.

'Look here. I've nothing to do with this. I'm a respectable citizen. Tomorrow I'm catching a ferry over to England. I'm starting a new job there. Why would I want to be involved in all this?'

He gestured with his arm to take in the area, the gunfire, the smoke, all that he was leaving behind. The soldier shouted,

'Shut the fuck up!'

He raised his rifle and hit Peter on the jaw. Peter fell to the ground dazed. He didn't feel any pain but was aware that something was flowing from his chin. He could see his shirtfront turning red and further red stains on his trousers. He felt nauseous and the world began to spin out of control. Hands grabbed him, men shouted in Scottish accents. They hauled him by his arms through the gap between the lorries and shoved him onto the floor of another army lorry, already full of men.

'Is that you, Peter? I thought you'd gone home,' he heard a familiar voice say.

What happened next was a blur. The lorry drove off and room was found for him on one of its benches. He kept slipping into unconsciousness and had to be propped up by the men on either side of him. He came to long enough to see that the lorry was driving into Crumlin Road Gaol. 'Not far from here to the house,' he thought. It was dark now and the cool night air jerked him awake. The gash on his jaw was still bleeding and he took his handkerchief out of his pocket and pressed it against the wound. Now he was in pain. There were soldiers all around the courtyard of the prison and they roughly herded the men through a large doorway. Inside they were told to line up. One by one they walked up to a desk where a prison warder sat, a large ledger in front of him. Peter could barely stand and the pain in his head was getting worse. Martin, his mate he'd been drinking with in what seemed another lifetime, had to hold him steady. After what seemed like an eternity, Peter stood in front of the warder who asked his name, address. Peter told him.

'Religion?'

'Irish Catholic,' Peter replied.

'No such religion. Roman Catholic,' the warder said pointedly.

'I need to see a doctor.' He took his bloodied handkerchief from his jaw. The blood started to flow again, 'See?'

'Not my department,' said the warder, 'Move on.'

The file of prisoners was led through a maze of corridors deeper into the prison by a body of hard-faced warders. It was full night now and the only light came from the bare bulbs hanging overhead, revealing the dingy walls and forbidding-looking metal doors. At the last corridor, cell doors were open and the men ordered to go inside. Peter and Martin were tolled off into a cell together. Built to accommodate four men in Victorian times there were six men in there already. Martin recognised some of them and they exchanged stories of how they were lifted. Peter, for whom space was made to sit on the edge of a bunk, thought the atmosphere was surprisingly cheerful.

'Do we get anything to eat?' a voice asked, 'I'm starving.'

'Aye, I'll just phone room service,' another voice answered.

Peter was beginning to come round, although he still was in great pain and felt woozy. His chief concern was getting to Leicester in time on Monday morning. If they let him out tomorrow, he could still get the ferry. He could go home first to wash and change his clothes. Luckily he had the sense to pack his bags already. Martin was standing next to him.

'Do you think they'll let us go tomorrow?' he asked.

Martin shook his head, 'I reckon it's internment. My Da was lifted back in the fifties and he spent a couple of years in Ballykinlar prison camp.'

Peter was stunned by this information. Just then, there was a rasping sound as the cover over the cell door's peephole was pulled back.

'Is there anyone in here requiring medical treatment?' a voice enquired.

'Aye, there's a man here in a bad way,' shouted Martin. 'Go on, Peter, get up.'

Outside Peter joined a line of men similar to himself, showing some sign of injury. One had a black eye, another held his arm painfully against his chest, a third was bleeding profusely from a head wound. Peter recognised one of them from a street in the Loney.

'Have you any idea what they're going to do to us?' he asked.

'I don't know. I'm –'

'No talking!' barked the warder.

Two warders, one in front, one behind, took them through more corridors until they came to a door marked 'Doctor'. They were told to stand there. The man with the head wound was called in first. After a few minutes, he came out with a bandage on his head and Peter was called in. The room was lined with glass-fronted cabinets containing bottles and medical equipment. A seedy, bald man badly in need of a shave sat at a desk covered in paper, medical dressings and bottles of different colours. The only thing to indicate that he was a doctor was the soiled white lab coat he wore over his open-necked shirt. He told Peter to sit down. As he sat down, Peter caught a glimpse of himself in a mirror. The gash in his jaw hung open like a fish's mouth and blood still oozed from it.

'That's a nasty cut, you have there,' said the man cheerily.

'Are you a doctor?' asked Peter.

'Medical orderly, but I can do the job. I'm going to have to stitch that.'

He took a curved needle, that appropriately enough reminded Peter of a fishhook, and a spool of thread from a tin box on the desk.

'Chin up,' said the MO.

Peter screeched as the needle entered his flesh.

'Can you not give me something to deaden the pain?'

'Sorry, we don't run to an anaesthetic.'

The MO didn't seem to be concerned at this deficiency. Peter got six stitches. He knew that, because he could feel every one going in. The MO stuck a plaster over the wound and gave him a couple of aspirin. Outside he waited with the group until the MO had seen to them all and then they were led back to their cells. Feeling slightly better, for the first time, Peter wondered just what he had got himself into.

He was not to know that he was caught up in the infamous Falls Road Curfew. The disturbances that he had witnessed quickly developed into gun battles between British soldiers and men from the IRA. The curfew would last for thirty-six hours as hundreds of British troops swamped the Falls. They carried out house-to-house searches for weapons, all the while coming under attack from the IRA and rioters. In return, the army fired CS gas and live rounds indiscriminately. Anyone who crossed them was liable to get rough treatment and many of the civilian population suffered at their hands. By the end, four locals were killed by the army and seventy-eight were wounded. Peter was one of the 337 men who were arrested.

On the British side, only eighteen soldiers were wounded. Those inside the prison, of course, could only speculate on what was happening.

Shortly after Peter's return to the cell, the door opened and a warder with a clip board demanded to know their names. Peter gladly gave his name but others only did so reluctantly. One man said, 'Seamus Ó Marcaigh.'

'What?' said the warder. The man repeated his name.

'Shamus O'Murky,' said the warder, writing that on his list.

They were left undisturbed for the rest of the night. They were given no food and had to make do as best they could for rest. Peter managed to wedge himself in a corner. He was so tired that he fell asleep, but kept waking up as he slipped away from the wall. Around him, some men also tried to sleep but most were too on edge. For most of the men, the greatest deprivation was the lack of cigarettes. The few they had between them soon ran out. The other shock was to discover that the white enamel bucket in the corner was their only toilet facility. Peter couldn't face using this with the other men watching, but by morning it was full to overflowing. Giving up on sleep, he looked at his fellow inmates. Some of them were subdued, in a huddle whispering to each other. Another group, among whom was Martin, discussed what to do when they got out.

'We'll have to get reorganised and rearmed.'

'I've heard there's training camps on the other side of the Border already.'

'Give us four or five months and we'll take the war to the British army.'

An elderly man who looked quite respectable in tweed jacket and corduroy trousers, sat on the edge of a bunk and told one filthy joke after another, much to the hilarity of those nearest him. Peter was shocked.

Morning eventually came and the cell door opened. A warder ordered them out and the whole corridor was led off. Soon Peter could smell food. In the canteen, he picked up a plastic tray from a table by the door and joined the queue. Despite warnings from the warders on duty, the prisoners exchanged greetings and opinions on what was going on back in the Falls. The food was dished out by men in dirty overalls from a counter like you'd see in a self-service restaurant with food in steel trays kept warm by powerful lamps. Breakfast consisted of a slice of fatty bacon, a rubbery fried egg and soggy toast. There were large pots of tea doing the rounds and Peter gladly had three cupfuls, even though it was strong and bitter. A whistle announced the end of breakfast and, as he left the canteen to follow the others back, a warder approached Peter.

'Are you Peter Hannon?' Peter nodded. 'Right, follow me. You've a visitor.'

Peter was elated by this. It must be Maggie. He was sure that she'd come to take him home. After all, he was a law-abiding citizen and this was all a mistake.

The warder led him to an interview room where a middle-aged man in a pinstriped suit was sitting. Peter looked about, expecting to see Maggie. The man rose and shook Peter's hand.

'I'm Charles Magowan, your solicitor.'

'Did my wife send you?'

'No, your mother.'

'My mother?' said Peter, surprised.

'Yes. A neighbour saw you being arrested and he told your mother about it, and she got on to me. I've known your mother for years. My office is in Lower Albert Street, the city centre end. I sometimes call in for a drink after work in the nearby pub. Your mother is often there with her circle of friends. She's quite chatty.'

All this was news to Peter.

'What's going to happen to me?' he asked.

'There's a special sitting of the magistrate's court on Monday morning. You'll be tried at that.'

'I have to be in Leicester on Monday,' Peter pleaded, 'I've a new job to go to.'

'Oh, there's no chance of that. Now tell me, in your own words, exactly what happened.'

As Peter recounted the events for Mr Magowan, he

suddenly remembered seeing someone he knew standing across the street while he was talking to the soldier.

'I have a witness who can prove I'm innocent. Tommy Crossan, an old neighbour of ours from Scotch Street. We grew up together. He can vouch for me.'

Magowan smiled and took a note of this.

'I'll see if I can contact him. And if he is willing to appear in court.'

'Tommy is something in the Post Office. He's respectable,' added Peter.

When he returned to the cell, Peter could see that there were only five people there. He noticed that Seamus Ó Marcaigh was no longer there.

'Not everybody came back from breakfast,' Martin explained, 'They took away the fellas they think are active. Not that they got all the right ones.'

'What'll happen to them?' asked Peter.

'God knows.'

When Peter told Martin about the solicitor and that they would be up before the magistrate on Monday, he said, 'Thank Christ for that!'

'What do you mean?' asked Peter.

'Don't you see? That means it's not internment. The worst we'll get is a week or two in prison and then we'll be out. Do you hear what Peter's saying, boys?'

Most people were happy that they weren't being interned but a couple, like Peter, weren't happy about spending any time in prison. How could he could explain that to the people in Leicester?

Things seemed a bit more organised now. Some of the other men were called out to meet their solicitors, but apart from that they were left undisturbed in their cells. At five o'clock they were brought to the canteen again for a meal of lumpy potatoes, over-boiled vegetables, and an unidentifiable meat. On Sunday morning, they were taken out to Mass, that is those who had identified themselves as Catholic. By now they had a clearer idea of what had been going on outside. There were whispered exchanges as word was passed from one pew to another while the priest intoned Mass. The news was met with a mixture of anger and relief. They were all angry that the army was running amok on the Falls, but many were happy to be out of it. Peter still had faith in law and order, so he was more subdued in his comments and harboured the hope that on Monday the magistrate would release him without a stain on his character. He would contact the people in Leicester to explain he was delayed. Everything would be alright.

After a night that was only slightly less comfortable than the previous one, the prisoners were taken out in groups to go to court. Names were called out by a warder and they were marched off in batches. Peter was in the third batch to go. As they reached the exit to the courtyard, he was handcuffed to another prisoner. He didn't recognise any of the others with him. He felt a primeval shudder when they were led into a dark, damp tunnel. After a couple of minutes, they emerged at the other end in the court building, across the road from the gaol. The courthouse on the Crumlin Road was a Belfast landmark. This large neo-Classical structure stood in elegant contrast to the brutal granite of the gaol. Peter had passed the courthouse hundreds of times driving up and down the Crumlin Road without giving it a second thought. He was disappointed to see no sign of Mr Magowan in the area where they had to wait to be called before the magistrate. At least the handcuffs were removed. He was full of nerves as one by one they were summoned into the courtroom. After the events of the previous forty-eight hours, the magistrate, an elderly gentleman, would have tried them as a job lot and sentenced them all to prison, but the proprieties had to be observed. By the time Peter appeared before him, he was feeling jaded.

He welcomed the sight of Mr Magowan, who was representing many of the men arrested on the Falls. He greeted Peter from his table with an enigmatic nod. After the charge was read out and Peter pleaded not guilty, the magistrate was about to pronounce sentence when Mr Magowan jumped to his feet and begged leave to present the defence. Looking nonplussed, the magistrate agreed. Magowan outlined the course of events as Peter had explained to him. To the magistrate's consternation, there was no military witness to present evidence, but he had to accept that the defence had a witness. Thomas Crossan, in suit and tie, entered the witness box and gave evidence that Peter Hannon was behaving in a peaceable manner and that the soldier in question had overreacted. Much to Peter's relief, the magistrate accepted Tommy at his word and the case was dismissed.

In the foyer of the courthouse, Maggie appeared out of the crowd of lawyers, relatives of the men inside, and journalists. She stood in front of him in stunned silence. Peter was in a sorry state. He had been wearing the same clothes for three days and had not had a wash or shave. The lack of sleep made his face sag, and then there was the bloody plaster on his chin. For once Maggie was subdued and lost for words. She could only say how glad she was to see him safe and a free man. She fussed over the plaster on his chin and would not accept his assurance that he was alright. She kept glancing nervously about as she hurriedly ushered him through the throng of people and out onto the street.

'I'm taking you straight home and giving you a good breakfast, and then you can take a bath. My God! If you could see yourself,' she said once they were inside their car.

As Maggie pulled into the drive, her sister Beth opened the front door. She had spent the night there, comforting Maggie who was imagining all sorts of terrible things being done to Peter. Finn was there too. His mother brought him along just in case a message had to be run, like getting eggs and milk from the local shop. Maggie rushed in the door with Peter in tow.

'My God!' she exclaimed. 'If you'd heard what Peter just told me. What he's been through. Those British bastards!'

Finn almost fell over with shock. He'd never heard Aunt Maggie use bad language before, and had never heard her criticise the British.

'Look at his face! Some soldier did that. And then they dragged him into the back of a lorry. Look at the blood on his shirt. He's lucky to be alive! If I had that wee skitter here, I'd do for him, I would.'

Finn could only look on in astonishment at this tirade from his aunt. She was like a different woman. 'The Bastards,' she said again. His mother was equally astonished and could only say the odd word of agreement.

They managed to calm Maggie down long enough to get Peter some breakfast that Finn's mother had cooked. He had said little or nothing since he came in, but over breakfast he recounted his adventure, as he called it. Finn thought it was like something from a war film. His mother crossed herself, saying, 'Jesus, Mary, and Joseph,' at each new revelation. After breakfast, Maggie ran a bath and insisted that Peter have a good long soak.

'We'll get Dr Coyle to have a look at that wound of yours. I'll phone him now.'

Finn was sent into the kitchen to wash the dishes while his mother and aunt had a cup of tea in the sitting room. However, he could hear every word they said. Maggie was calmer by now but still angry.

'What about the job?' he heard his mother ask. 'Isn't Peter supposed to be in Leicester today?'

'Oh that. I don't think we want to be in England now. Sure they hate us Irish.'

Finn had to laugh at this. The number of times he'd heard Aunt Maggie go on about how everything was great in England.

'You can't be like that, Maggie. You can't judge them all on what's happened to Peter. You said yourself, it's a great opportunity. Peter will be earning good money,' his mother reasoned.

Maggie was emphatic in response, 'The way I feel now, seeing the state of him and that gash on his chin, I wouldn't let Peter take that job at all. No matter how much they paid him!'

— III —

The School Tie

FINN HAD WORKED HARD to get his Eleven Plus. Passing that exam would mean a scholarship to go to a grammar school. It was already decided that if he passed he would go to St Malachy's College, not just the closest to where he lived but one of the most prestigious in Ireland. His father, Pat, had got some past papers and every night when he came home from work, even before they'd had their dinner, he would sit down with Finn and coach him in answering the questions. His dad had left school when he was fourteen and gone to work for his uncle who owned a small building firm. Even so, he loved learning and was always reading books. He was determined that Finn would get the chances that he never had. In his final year at primary school, he discouraged Finn from spending his free time hanging around with his pals or playing games out in the street. Finn was unhappy with this and lost touch with some of his best friends, but he thought too much of his dad to defy him. Despite this extra coaching, Finn was nervous about the exam, afraid that he would let down his parents. Only a handful of boys in the class were expected to pass the Eleven Plus, even though every boy had to sit it. Finn was one of those whom his teacher, Mr O'Gorman, was sure would pass the exam, but he put the fear of God into all the boys, including Finn, urging them to study and to take the exam seriously.

The school Finn went to was officially called St Columbanus's, but it was known to all as Sacred Heart primary school after the parish church. There were forty-two pupils in Finn's P7 year, divided into two classes, one under Mr Armstrong, and his class under Mr O'Gorman. Mr O'Gorman was a good teacher who knew how to encourage the bright students, educate the not-so-bright, and keep the rowdy ones under control. He had no illusions about who would pass the Eleven Plus, and the seven that he predicted were the boys who got the scholarship. In this working-class area, it was no surprise that so few made it. In fact the parents of one boy who passed the exam wouldn't let him go on to grammar school, his father proudly declaring that it wasn't for the likes of them. Of the five or so streets off Manor Street which had Catholic families in them, only Finn and another boy, Conor Scott, passed the Eleven Plus. Conor lived in one of the slightly better houses on Manor Street and his father worked at a clerical job in the central post office so it was not so surprising that he was going to St Malachy's.

Finn started in St Malachy's College in September 1969. The Troubles had been going on for over a year by then and, although Finn's neighbourhood was relatively quiet, there was widespread violence across the North. But for Finn, the only thing that mattered was passing the Eleven Plus. That summer for him had been all about getting into St Malachy's. He and his parents had to be interviewed by the college president and when he gave his approval, there were lists of books to be bought along with sports gear and, of course, the all-important uniform. Pat and Beth, his parents, were over the moon that he had got into the college and were determined that he would not be found wanting in front of the other boys from posh families. So, despite the expense, they not only got him the trousers, blazer, pullover, and tie, but also a skullcap with the college badge and even a scarf in the college colours of green, white, and black. The unveiling of the uniform was a big event with his aunts there to see what he looked like, and then he had to model it for his grannies the following Saturday when they went for their usual visit to their houses on the Falls Road. Beneath his embarrassment at all this, Finn was proud of his uniform and thought he looked good in it.

Going from a small primary school to the 'big' school was a frightening experience. Finn was glad that Conor and three other pals from Sacred Heart PS were going with him. But he

soon fell into a routine. He left his house at 8:30 and called
for Conor who lived round the corner. They walked along
Manor Street to the Cliftonville Road where they waited for
another pal who lived further up the road. If he wasn't there,
which he sometimes wasn't, they hung on for a while and if he
didn't show up, went on to the college without him. On the
way down Cliftonville Road, the boys had to pass the mock
Scottish baronial building of Belfast Royal Academy, known
as BRA. This was older than St Malachy's and considered
by some to be more prestigious. Unlike St Malachy's which
was a good twenty minutes or more away, BRA was just a
brief walk from Finn's house, but it was a Protestant grammar
school, which meant that Finn and his pals couldn't go there.
Coming home wasn't the same process in reverse as Finn had
been put into a different class from his friends which meant
he sometimes finished at a different time from them, or they
might be involved in some after-school activity. So often he
would make his way back home on his own.

On the corner of Manor Street and the Cliftonville Road
was a sweet shop, the type that does not exist anymore. It sold
sweets of all kinds from penny chews to luxurious boxes of
chocolates. To look in its window was like getting a glimpse
of paradise with its array of chocolate bars, shiny boxes tied
up with ribbons, and jars of boiled sweets. If on his own,
Finn would always take time to look at the shop window. He
had a sweet tooth and would daydream about what he might
buy. His father gave him his pocket money on Friday but it
was never enough to buy the elegant rich sweets that were so
prominently displayed in the window. Finn had to be satisfied
with something like a Mars bar or loose sweets in a paper
bag.

One day on the way home from school, Finn was engaged
in his daydreaming at the shop window when another boy
in school uniform came up beside him. He too stopped and
began to look longingly in at the marvellous array of sweets.
Like Finn, he wore grey trousers and a black school blazer. He
had a wee black skullcap on his head. Finn had one of those
too but it was back home in his bedroom. The cap was listed

as an item of school uniform and his parents had purchased one. His mammy insisted he wear it for fear he might get into trouble, but on his first day at school, he soon found out that only himself and a handful of other new boys wore the skullcap. After a few quizzical remarks and jokes from older boys, his cap was whipped off and put safely out of sight in his schoolbag. So Finn felt sorry for this boy being forced to wear his skullcap even out of school.

Finn did not recognise him but since he had only been at St Malachy's a few weeks and there were hundreds of boys of similar age, it was no surprise that he couldn't place him. The other boy opened the conversation by asking Finn what were his favourite sweets. Finn and he exchanged notes on the quality of various brands and types of chocolate. From his comments, Finn realised that the other boy was better off, as he talked about actually buying some of the more expensive sweets. The conversation turned to how they were getting on in the 'big school'. They soon discovered that they both had the same anxieties and observations about being in a school with hundreds of students and a different teacher for each subject. When they started discussing teachers in detail, Finn realised that something was not quite right. None of the names the other boy mentioned rang a bell with him, not even if he used their nicknames. Feeling curious, Finn sneaked a glance at the boy. His uniform looked just like his, but a closer inspection revealed that he was not from St Malachy's at all. His tie was in the BRA colours of navy blue and red. The badge on his blazer pocket was a BRA badge.

Finn was surprised that this boy would talk with him but glad that he did. Apart from elderly neighbours in his street, Finn didn't know any Protestants. Even though his parents were conscientiously anti-sectarian, the unwritten laws of Belfast dictated that Catholic and Protestant children did not mix. But he was still full of adventurous spirit from starting at a new school and thought that the chance to meet a Protestant, perhaps even become friends, was part of the experience of being a big boy at a big school. He wondered what he could say to move the conversation on.

However the BRA boy had also twigged that something was not right. He suddenly stopped talking and turned to examine Finn properly. His eyes went from Finn's trousers to his blazer, rested briefly on his school badge, and then settled on Finn's green, white, and black tie. The look on his face would stay with Finn forever. It was one of shock, fear, and disgust.

The BRA boy took a step back as if stung by a wasp. He began to speak, 'You – you're a... a...'

He could not complete the sentence but Finn knew what he meant: he was a Catholic, a Taig. Before Finn could say another word, the BRA boy turned on his heel and hurried off. Finn took a step forward, his hand out, but it was too late. The BRA boy ran across the Cliftonville Road and into one of the side streets that would take him to a Protestant district.

In the weeks that followed, whenever Finn passed a group of BRA boys, he looked out for the boy from the sweet shop. He hoped that they might get to know each other. He felt this was an opportunity that he should not let slip by. Once, he thought he recognised him among a group standing round the gates into BRA. Their eyes locked for a second and then the boy turned away with no sign of acknowledgement. And Finn gave up on his search.

IV

Border Crossing

MOIRA, HIS WIFE, had been at her sister Sarah's house in Belfast for over a week now. She went to stay there as soon as news came that her brother-in-law, Jim, would not survive the latest bout of illness. He had been ill for so long now that it almost came as a relief when definite news came. Paul was fond of Jim in the way that you are for a brother-in-law and had always enjoyed his company. He had felt sad when Sarah had first phoned from Belfast to say that Jim was unwell, and worse when told he had only a year or two left. However, as it dragged on with one episode after another and false alarms that had sent them scuttling from Dublin to Belfast at short notice, Paul was beginning to think of Jim as a nuisance and secretly hoped that he would just die and be done with it. That would be the decent thing to do.

So when Moira phoned to say that he had passed away Paul was relieved. He said all the things Moira wanted to hear and was mightily glad that Sarah, the sister, was too upset to speak to him.

'The funeral's on Thursday,' she said, 'You'd best come up on Wednesday if you can get the time off work.'

'That'll be no problem.' He heard Moira speak to someone in the room, heard her say, 'Right, OK', and then turn back to him, 'And Paul, there's one more thing. You'll have to come up with Séan. You know what he's like about travelling. And you can pick up Tom on the way through Ardee. And, Paul, don't forget your black tie.'

'That's three things,' he joked. 'Do those two know I'm coming for them or do I have to phone?'

'Ach, you'll have to phone.'

Moira and her big family, he thought. Séan, another

brother-in-law, he didn't mind. Séan's own wife, Moira's older sister, had died some years before, and even Moira called Séan the 'merry widower'. He'd borne his grief well and, as a man should, thought Paul, got on with life. He was good company and at sixty-six, about ten years older than Paul, was still game and could give younger men a run for their money when it came to drinking or partying. It was not that he was the life and soul of the party but he enjoyed the craic and always had a fund of jokes to tell. Paul wouldn't mind travelling up to Belfast with him.

Tom was another matter. Paul was never sure of just where he fitted into the family. In the thirty years he'd been married to Moira he had met Tom about a dozen times at family gatherings, like weddings or funerals. He was variously referred to as a cousin or uncle. His mother had died when he was a child and he'd been sent by his father to live with an aunt of Moira's and her husband. That meant he was a de facto uncle to some, cousin to others. Paul didn't really care. It was just that Tom was difficult to get along with. He was a dour, taciturn man whom it was difficult to get a conversation out of. He lived on his own and it appeared like he had never had a woman in his life. Paul could not even talk work with him as he didn't know how exactly Tom made a living in Ardee. Like a lot of people in the country, he did some dealing in whatever was going. One time he might talk about buying and selling cattle, another time it might be trading in used cars.

Early on Wednesday morning, Paul stood in front of the hall mirror and checked that he had the car key, money, and his driving licence. He would need that if they were crossing the Border. A little later he arrived outside Séan's house which was not too far away. He had just switched off the engine when Séan came bounding down the steps and along the garden path with a plastic suit bag over his shoulder and a small overnight bag in his hand. It did not take them long to cross the city and get onto the N2 heading north for Ardee. Paul was secretly proud of his car. It was a big black Audi that was comfortable to travel in and gave acceleration when you needed it. He steered it with an easy confidence and smoothly overtook slower vehicles on the road. So with Séan chatting away beside him in the passenger seat, the time passed easily. The many little villages and towns on the way came and went almost unnoticed, and before they knew it they were in Ardee's main street.

As arranged, Tom was standing outside the big pub on the left. Paul noticed that he was already wearing a dark suit and black tie, with no sign of an overnight bag. With a nod and a smile he opened the door and lowered himself into the back seat. He was not a tall man and had the comfortable all-over fat of the well-off. Glancing in the rear-view mirror at Tom in his large round glasses, ensconced in the middle of the seat, Paul thought he looked like a sleek mole.

'Hope you weren't waiting long, Tom.'

'Not a bother, Paul. Only just got here. To tell you the truth, I was running a bit late. A few last-minute calls to make.'

Tom's telegraphic style was in contrast to Séan who greeted Tom with a welcome, a short peroration on the weather, and a reminiscence of a similar pick-up that went wrong – 'Although that was on the way to a wedding, not a funeral. Me and the wife had been asked to pick up this fella on our way to the church which was in Howth so it was quite a trek in those days. Anyway, didn't we arrive bright and early outside Mulligan's on Poolbeg Street and no sign of yer man, O'Reilly I think his name was. Thinking he was just delayed we hung on for a while. It was a lovely June morning as I recall, the sunlight glistening off the Liffey, hardly a soul about. Well after three-quarters of an hour, we began to get worried. If we didn't leave soon we'd miss the wedding altogether, but what to do? There was no houses nearby and all the shops were closed. Besides, I couldn't see a phone-box anywhere and it was too early for the pub to be open. So in the end we went off without him. I'm telling you there was a terrible fuss at the church from the sister-in-law, the bride's mother as it happened. But sure it wasn't our fault. And didn't yer man, O'Reilly, show up in a taxi as we were all traipsing out of the church after the wedding? The bloody eejit had been waiting outside Alfie Mulligan's on Stephen's Green the whole time!'

By the time Séan finished his story, the car had already left Ardee and was on the road to Dundalk where they had decided to stop for lunch, although there was nowhere worth eating in the place except the Imperial Hotel, but they did not want to stop anywhere in the North just in case. Lunch was pleasant enough. Steak pie and chips all round, washed down with a pint of Guinness. By two o'clock they were back in the car and off again.

Paul pulled off the main road at Ballymascanlon explaining, 'I'm not going to take the main road. That checkpoint outside Newry is always busy and we'd be stuck there for an hour or more. Going through Carlingford is longer in miles but the checkpoint at the Border is a quiet wee place and we'll be through it in no time.'

Tom said he had no idea about this part of the world and Séan agreed with Paul that this way would save time in the long run.

The day had turned out nice. One of those days on the cusp of winter and spring that was bright and sunny although cold. It was pleasant to be off the main road and driving along this quiet country road. Dundalk Bay stretched out on their right and the Cooley mountains rose on their left. The sunlight bounced off the neat dry stone walls, trees swayed in the breeze. And there were even a few spring lambs gambolling around their mothers. Just like a John Hinde postcard, thought Paul. It was all very pleasant driving along like this. There was not much traffic on the road, just the occasional tractor or cart that Paul easily overtook. The car was full of good humour as Séan told one amusing anecdote after another, or made funny observations about the houses and people they passed. You would not think that they were going to a funeral at all. And this thought made Paul feel a bit guilty. After all Jim wasn't a bad man, and Paul was fond of him in a way. He felt he should say something to the other two to remind them of why they were together, but the atmosphere was too good to interrupt.

It was as they neared Omeath after going through
Carlingford that Paul began to have an uneasy feeling. He
always did when heading North. He and Moira had already
left Belfast for London when the Troubles started fifteen
years before in 1968. So he had not experienced it at firsthand
but he'd followed events on the television and had family and
friends to tell him what it was really like living through it.
They'd moved to Dublin from England three years ago when
Paul got the promotion and they'd both been back in Belfast a
few times since then. Paul never liked going there. His family
and friends in the city had told him stories of army brutality,
of the daily harassment at checkpoints, the house searches and
so on. And of course, there was Bloody Sunday and other
cases of the Brits shooting people down. He reassured himself
that they were three respectable middle-aged, or older, men
on their way to a funeral. What could they be suspected of?
He was sure that the soldiers on the checkpoint would just
wave them through.

The checkpoint was a huge green and black structure that
straddled the canal road to Newry just after the Border, a
sangar the army called it. Once you were in it, you could see
nothing but concrete and corrugated iron walls looming over
you. These were painted in green and black camouflage, while
the barbed wire and camouflage netting obscured any possible
view of the world beyond. Paul gave what he hoped was a
disarming smile and rolled down the window as he slowed
the car to a halt beside the soldier in the middle of the road.
The young private smiled back in a tight perfunctory way. He
was dressed like the walls in the camouflage pattern green and
black, with a dark beret on his head. In his arms he cuddled
his SLR rifle, like it was something delicate. 'Any ID, Sir?' he
asked in an accent that Paul placed as Yorkshire. He'd been up
that way a few times over the years in the course of his work.
Paul handed over his driving licence. The soldier awkwardly
turned the pages while trying to keep his rifle balanced as he
examined each one. He stared for what seemed like minutes
at Paul's photograph. The three men in the car stared in
silence at the soldier in turn. Tom had never been through a

checkpoint before and was nervous. Séan had gone through the experience before and displayed the nonchalance of an old hand. Tom coughed nervously and pulled at his collar.

'Just a minute. Turn off your engine and wait,' the soldier said and walked away. He went in through a steel door in the side of the checkpoint and out of sight. There were no other soldiers to be seen and all was silent except for a faint rumble of voices, and the occasional crackle of a radio. The minutes ticked slowly past. A couple of other cars came into the checkpoint. A different soldier appeared and, after a cursory glance at the driver's ID, he directed them past Paul's car and sent them on their way. Another soldier appeared from nowhere and stationed himself a few feet away from the car, his rifle trained on Paul. Paul was convinced that he was aiming his SLR directly at his head.

Suddenly the first soldier reappeared. 'Start your engine and move the car over there,' he ordered tersely. Paul steered the car across the road and through a gap in the checkpoint wall. He found himself in kind of tunnel created by corrugated iron sheeting. The exit was closed off and the only light came from two powerful lamps mounted on tripods. A shadow emerged out of the glare and a bereted head was stuck into the car, face to face with Paul.

'What did you say your business was in Belfast?' the newcomer asked.

Although he was dressed just like the other young soldier and was about the same age, the clipped accent so familiar from British war films gave him away as an officer. Paul explained about the funeral. The fresh-faced officer looked dubious. He stared at each of them in turn before saying curtly, 'Right. Everybody out of the car – Now.'

As the three respectable men in suits climbed stiffly out of the car, the young officer said, 'Sergeant, take these men to the interrogation room.' Out of the shadows a sergeant and three other soldiers came into view, pointing their rifles at them. With a grunt the sergeant took Paul's shoulder and pushed him towards an opening in the corrugated iron and forced him down a dimly lit corridor to a windowless room.

The other two were manhandled in the same way.

The room had no windows. The light was provided by two bare fluorescent strips hanging from the ceiling. The glare was already giving Paul a headache. He looked round at Tom and Séan. They were both confused and frightened. Séan's usual smile and twinkle in the eye were gone. 'It'll be all right,' said Paul. 'No talking!' barked the sergeant. The officer, looking even younger and more fresh-faced in this light, came in and sat behind the desk gesturing for them to sit down too. Like three naughty schoolboys hauled up before the headmaster, Paul, Tom, and Séan sat down meekly on the three plastic office chairs that the sergeant had pulled in front of the desk. He went back to the door and stood on guard. Two other soldiers stood behind them, rifles at the ready. The officer took out a clipboard on which were some sheets of paper and carefully set it on the desk.

'Now,' he said as he searched inside his camouflage jacket before extracting a very ordinary ballpoint pen, 'let's begin again from the beginning. We'll start with you,' indicating Paul. 'Name? Address? Purpose of visit? When do you propose to leave Ulster?'

Feeling rather annoyed, Paul gave his name and address, explained again about the funeral and when they would be coming home. The procedure was repeated with Tom and Séan who were both nervous and stumbled over their answers.

'Why did you come by this road?' the officer asked.

'To avoid the traffic. There's always a hold-up at the checkpoint on the main Dublin road.' Paul felt foolish as he said it. In these circumstances, he thought it made him sound petulant.

'I see,' the officer replied enigmatically.

There was a moment's silence interrupted when another soldier, conspicuous for being unarmed and bareheaded, knocked at the door and came in. Paul recognised his driving licence in his hand. He handed the licence to the officer and whispered in his ear. The officer nodded in reply and the soldier left.

'Would you mind emptying your pockets?' the officer

suddenly said. With no word of protest they began to do so. Feeling even more like a naughty schoolboy in front of the headmaster, Paul started with his jacket pockets, and took out a pocket diary, a fountain pen, his keys, an old envelope that he had forgotten was there, and a neat clean handkerchief. He took some coins and his wallet out of his trousers and placed these on the desk in front of the officer with the rest of his possessions. Séan went through the same routine and his haul was almost identical to Paul's: a pocket diary, a ballpoint pen, keys, a clean handkerchief, coins and a wallet. They both turned their heads to observe Tom. He was in a dither. He tried one pocket and then another of his jacket, apparently coming up empty. Going to his trouser pockets, he too pulled out a wallet, a bunch of keys, and some coins, and put them on the desk. Then going back to his inside jacket pocket he removed a diary and a wad of used envelopes which he also put on the desk. After what seemed like minutes, he reached into the side pockets of his jacket. The left one was empty but from the right one he extracted a handkerchief, a dirty, crumpled specimen. It may have once been white but now it was faded grey colour. It looked as though it had not been washed or ironed in months. It was totally disreputable. Tom gingerly placed it on the desk alongside his other belongings.

The officer skimmed through the diaries and wallets. He took the letters out of the envelopes but only glanced at them. He picked up their keys and examined them closely as if they might reveal some secret. The coins he sorted into neat piles. He unfolded Paul's and then Séan's handkerchiefs, looked at them and placed them unfolded back on the desk. Picking up his pen, he poked at Tom's sad decrepit handkerchief. He stabbed at it as if trying to unfold it and then flipped it back at Tom with a snort of contempt.

'Righto. You can go,' he said. He leaned back in his chair while the sergeant opened the door and gestured with his thumb for them to follow him. Soon they were back in the car and Paul started the engine. With relief they emerged out of the other end of the tunnel into daylight. Accelerating quickly, Paul drove off in the direction of Newry.

The three of them were silent. It was like being mugged, Paul thought. He was not sure what was worse about the experience. Was it being taken into the heart of the checkpoint not knowing what was going to happen to you? Or was it being treated with contempt by a youngster who had barely begun shaving? He shivered and clutched the wheel more tightly, wishing that he could drive faster. He sensed the others felt the same, and thought that you could cut the silence with a knife. As they neared the outskirts of Newry, Séan broke the tension, 'I think we could do with a stiff drink after that.'

They sat in the comforting darkness of a bar. The wood panelling and brass fittings seemed homely, friendly even, after the army sangar. They had found a quiet corner where Paul and Séan sat on one side of the table, Tom on the other, each with a whiskey in front of him. Apart from deciding on what to drink, they still hadn't spoken to each other.

Again it was Séan who spoke first when he made a crack about this being a bonding experience. Paul gave a forced laugh in return. Awkwardly clearing his throat, Tom said, 'I do *have* clean hankies.'

V

A Trip to the Seaside

FINN WAS FIDDLING with the tuner on the car radio, trying to find some pop music. His cousin Ray was driving fast and confidently through the streets. Finn didn't see much of Ray lately. He was his cousin and a few years older than him. Somehow they'd remained friends even though Finn was a bookish grammar-school boy and Ray a plumber who struggled to read comics – not that he had a literacy problem, just lacked the patience. Ray was the son of Finn's Aunt Bridie. When they got burned out of their house, they moved in with Finn's parents for a few weeks while the Housing Executive found them somewhere to live. Ray had moved into Finn's bedroom and since then he was more like a kind of older brother to Finn. In any case the extended Conlyn clan were all pretty close and the two cousins did most of their growing up together. They had seen a lot of each other when younger. Ray was nearing the end of his time in primary school when Finn was starting there and had looked after him until he settled in. Pat, Finn's father, and Uncle Barney, Bridie's husband, had bought a ramshackle house together just across the Border. Their two families, along with those of Finn's other uncle, Christy, and their sister, Rosie, spent summer holidays there.

The house became a bolthole for all of them. It was a place they could escape the Troubles. As children they would cheer when they crossed the Border, glad to be in the Republic, which meant freedom in so many ways. Later the Border crossing became more fraught as the British Army positioned a permanent checkpoint on the road. Crossing the Border became an ordeal. Sometimes, the car was just waved through with no problem. Mostly they were held up while everyone's identity was checked and the soldiers satisfied themselves that they were all telling the same story. However, now and again, they would get some awkward sergeant or officer who would make them all get out of the car. This was quite a sight as the driver was the only one who had a seat to himself, so three or more adults and up to seven children might crawl out of the old estate, and there might be a dog too. They would have to stand by the side of the road while squaddies searched the car, opened boxes and suitcases, and even took out the back seat. After it had all been put back in, they recreated the acrobatic manoeuvres required to fit them back in the car. The experience at the Border became a sort of ritual, a rite of passage. If it went well and they got through OK, they took this as a sign that the holiday would be good. There was also a Garda checkpoint on the other side of the Border but they usually just waved them through.

The old country house wasn't much to look at, just a plain white-washed three-room cottage, but it was like a second home to the children, and the district around was their kingdom. To them, it was a place of adventure which they explored, played games in, and fought wars. They renamed the fields and hills around the house. There was the Fort (a ruined farmhouse), the Badlands (a small wood on the mountainside), the hideout (a clearing amid a tangle of thorn bushes and brambles). Even though it had no electricity or running water, the Conlyns made it a place of comfort. They fetched water from a nearby well – it was a sign that you were one of the big kids when you could carry a bucket of water to the house – installed gas lighting, and fetched firewood from wherever they could find it. The whole clan became a feature in the area and, for the people in the surrounding farms and the pub on the main road, summer only began when the first of the Conlyns arrived.

As Finn and his cousins grew older, they made their way independently to the house. When he was sixteen, Ray and a mate had got there once through a combination of buses and lifts and turned up unexpectedly on the doorstep. Uncle Christy was very obliging in driving the older kids down to the house and fetching them again when the weekend was over. Once Ray got a car of his own, trips to the house were more frequent. Sometimes they would drive down, not to visit the house but to spend the day in Omeath, the nearest village. Of course, the house was there if they needed to stay overnight.

That was what was happening now. It was May and the weather had been good all week. Out of the blue, Ray had contacted Finn to say that he was going to Omeath on Saturday and did Finn want to come along. Ever since Finn's father died four years previously, Ray had been good in seeing that Finn had his share of fun. Finn's mother was left shattered by the death and, in any case, had always been a home bird. Left to her, Finn and his brother and sister would have spent most of their time at home apart from two weeks' summer holiday. Finn's mother could not see that a teenage boy needed to be out and about, had to learn about life and get to meet girls. Ray took it on himself to show Finn how to be a teenager. In truth, Finn was not too adventurous himself. He was shy with girls, not much good at sports, and was just as happy to sit at home with a book. But he liked and admired Ray and had to admit that he had a good time, mostly, when he invited him along on one his outings.

Ray turned onto the Antrim Road. This was not the most direct route to the Falls Road but that way was blocked by so-called Peace Walls, built to keep the Catholics and Protestants apart. One had been built dividing Manor Street in two and effectively giving the River Street Loyalists control of a few streets that used to be mixed Protestant and Catholic. There were more walls separating the Protestant Shankill Road from the Catholic Falls where some of the worst street fighting had taken place in the early days of the Troubles. Now they had to drive onto Clifton Street and then across the bottom of the Shankill Road to reach the Falls Road. They managed to do this without meeting an army or RUC checkpoint, much to their relief. Two young men in a car driving from North Belfast to the Falls could expect hassle if stopped at a checkpoint. Ray drove the short distance up the Falls Road to the Divis Flats and parked the car in front of one of the blocks.

'I'll only be a minute,' he said as he got out of the car. 'Oh, and you'll have to get in the back seat.'

Finn moved into the back seat and waited. It was about ten minutes before Ray reappeared. Finn had sat nervously as a few people who passed by stared suspiciously at him. Out on the road an army patrol, two Land Rovers, drove by. Out of each one, the head and shoulders of a soldier could be seen, training his rifle in different directions. When one pointed his SLR in Finn's direction, he expected the patrol to swerve off the road and check him out. He breathed a sigh of relief when the Land Rovers drove on past. You never knew where an encounter with the Brits might lead.

Ray appeared out of the entrance to the flats. He had Sheila with him. Ray was never short of girlfriends and sometimes seemed to be dating two at the same time, but Sheila was different. He'd been with her a couple of months now and was not cheating on her – as far as Finn knew. Sheila was a tall blonde and Finn thought she was beautiful. Today she was wearing a white T-shirt that clung to her figure, revealing the curve of her breasts, and a pair of tight jeans. 'Venus in blue jeans,' Finn said to himself when he saw her. He was in awe of Sheila and a little in love with her himself. He did not realise the she was in awe of him. She had never known anyone who was as intelligent as him or who read so many books. The fact that he had nine O-Levels and would be starting his A-Levels in September and go on to university really impressed her. No one in her family had got very far in education and no one really read books. All the men had ended up in labouring jobs. Sometimes she teased Finn for being a brainiac but really she loved talking to him; his conversation was always interesting.

''Bout ye, Finn?' she said when she got into the car. 'Are you looking forward to our day at the seaside?'

'I sure am. It'll be nice to get out of the city.'

'Right, then. Let's go,' said Ray, putting the car into gear and driving off.

It didn't take long to get onto Northern Ireland's only motorway, the M1, and start heading for the country. The sun was rising higher now as the morning wore on, and there was hardly a cloud in the sky. Ray's Ford Escort raced along in the overtaking lane, passing all the slow vehicles in the other lane. The RUC had other things to worry about than someone breaking the speed limit. The radio blared out pop music from Radio One and they all nodded their heads along with the rhythm. Every now and again Sheila turned to Finn in the back seat and gave him a smile. They turned off the motorway onto a two-lane road going south. Until recently the car would have had to pass through every little town and village on the way, making the journey to the Border a major trek, but by-passes had been built around most of them and so they could expect to reach Newry in about an hour and a half. David Bowie came on the radio singing 'Sorrow'. Ray turned to Sheila and started singing the chorus along with Bowie —

> With your long blonde hair
> And your eyes of blue
> The only thing I ever got from you
> Was sorrow ...

Sheila joined in, and Finn sang along too. Sheila looked the part alright with her long blonde hair and eyes of blue.

When they got to Newry, the town nearest the Border, Sheila turned the volume of the radio down a couple of notches.

'That's enough of that. Let's just enjoy the drive and the scenery.'

Ray grunted but did not put up an argument. He kept his eyes on the road as Newry was a tricky place to get through and always seemed to have a traffic jam. They joined the line of traffic heading south and had to crawl along.

'Do you know anything about Newry, Finn? It's my first time here,' said Sheila.

Finn give a little laugh, 'Every time we drive through here, our granny always says it's a very old town. Every time, like we'd never heard it before.'

'Is it?' she asked.

'Oh aye. It's said that St Patrick founded it. It was a big bustling town when Belfast was still a village, and the canal we're crossing over is the oldest in Ireland.'

'Gosh, you know just about everything about everything. Doesn't he, Ray?'

'Oh yeah, a right little brain-box is our Finn.'

'So what happened?' Sheila asked.

'Happened?' repeated Finn.

'Aye, why's Belfast a big city now and Newry's a wee town.'

'I don't know. I suppose Belfast just grew faster.'

'Oh, something you don't know,' said Sheila.

'I'll tell you what,' interrupted Ray. 'Newry's a Catholic town. It was starved of investment.'

This was the first time that Finn had heard Ray say anything that was vaguely political.

Once out of Newry and on the road that ran alongside the ship canal, Ray put his foot down again and the Ford Escort flew along. Finn loved this. He loved being in the country. His vision wasn't hemmed in by streets and the air smelled sweet. He loved seeing the sun glisten off the water of the canal, and seeing birds fly overhead. It felt like chains had been lifted off his body and he could move and breathe freely. He was glad he had accepted Ray's invitation to come along. They all rolled their windows down and fresh air blew around the car. Sheila's hair whirled around her head and she laughed.

Ray let out a yelp, 'This is the life!'

There were no other cars about and they felt like kings of the road.

'You'd better slow down, Ray,' cautioned Finn, 'The Brit checkpoint is just ahead.'

'Fuck them!' said Ray, but he slowed down as they approached the bend in the road.

The checkpoint came into view. There were jeeps on both sides of the road and sandbag emplacements occupied by soldiers with machine guns. Signs in the centre of the road warned motorists to slow down, switch off their headlights, and then to stop. Ray rolled down his window as the car slowly approached the soldier in full battle dress holding up his hand. Sheila switched off the radio. Awkwardly cradling his long rifle, the soldier leaned into the car. He looked at each of them in turn. He was young, probably not much older than Ray although it was difficult to tell as the full military kit of flak jacket and helmet gave him a menacing appearance. His eyes lingered on Sheila; his lust was almost palpable.

'Driver's licence,' he said.

'Will you get it out of the glove compartment, Sheila?' Ray asked.

'Sheila, is it?' said the Brit, 'a pretty name for a pretty girl.'

Sheila ignored him and Ray held his tongue. In the back seat, Finn felt anger swelling up inside him. How dare this foreign soldier insult her. But he too said nothing. Sheila pulled out old envelopes, a map and the remains of Ray's packed lunch from the day before.

'I can't find it, love,' she said nervously. They all knew the consequences if Ray couldn't produce his licence.

'It's in there,' said Ray with some anxiety.

'Oh, here it is!'

Sheila handed the licence to Ray who held it out to the soldier. He looked at it one page at a time.

'Well, Raymond, what are you doing on this road?'

'My Da has a house down here. A neighbour phoned to say he thought a slate had come off the roof. My Da asked me to check.'

'And Sheila here, she's a roofer is she?'

Ray sighed and held back an expletive,

'She's my girlfriend. She just came along for the day out.'

'Oh, so you're not married love? Any chance you'd come out with me?'

'Not in a million years,' Sheila spat back at him.

'I can always dream,' said the soldier lasciviously. 'OK, Paddy, here's your licence. See you on the way back, sweetheart.'

They sat in silence as they drove on down the road towards Omeath. It was not that the soldier had really said or done anything that was bad, but he had all the power, and his teasing had a nasty edge to it. They all knew what Brits were capable of. Sheila turned on the radio again and put it up loud, as if the cheery music would dispel the gloomy atmosphere that now permeated the car.

Ray responded as she hoped. 'Fuck them Brits. We're here to have fun!'

'Too damn right,' Sheila said ruffling his hair. 'Isn't that right Finn boy?'

'Too damn right,' he echoed.

Omeath was a wee seaside village of two streets. One ran up from the seafront and joined the other one that was part of the road that eventually led to Dundalk. Even though it was a sunny Sunday afternoon, the village was not very busy. A few people walked about, making the best of the sunshine, and there were a few cars parked along the streets. They mostly had Northern registration numbers. Omeath was a popular spot with Catholics from the North who wanted to escape the Troubles for a day. Ray had no problem finding a parking spot near the jetty where the ferry from Warrenpoint, in County Down, part of Northern Ireland, operated.

'You should have seen this place before the Troubles,' Ray told Sheila. 'It would have been hopping on a day like this. Isn't that right, Finn? You could barely move for the crowds and this street would have been lined with stalls selling all sorts of sweets and toys.'

'I've still got a tin spaceship my granny bought me when I was a wee boy,' said Finn.

'Ach you always were her favourite,' Ray joked. 'Have you ever sucked on a Peggy's Leg, Sheila?'

'What are you on about?' said Sheila blushing.

'Don't get your dander up. It's a wee stick of brown rock. Lovely it is. There used to be an old woman sat at the bottom of the hotel steps sold them out of a basket. Getting one of them was a real treat.'

They couldn't find a Peggy's Leg but a van was selling ice cream and they all got 99s. They sat on the low seawall and ate their ice cream cones. The incident at the Border was forgotten and they all enjoyed their 99s with the delight of children. Finn thought that this was the epitome of a good time: beautiful weather, the seaside and good company. Of course, it would have been better if he had a girlfriend of his own, but he never did have much luck with girls. He was shy around them and never knew the right things to say to win them over. He had found that showing off his knowledge of history, geography, or literature did not impress the girls he knew. Some were put off by his learning and the rest thought he was daft.

Not that he would say any of this to Ray or Sheila. As a teenager now, Omeath did not seem such an exciting place to Finn. There was definitely less to it, no stalls or buskers, no shooting galleries or donkey rides on its pebbly beach. It may have lost its magic but it still had its charm. The scenery was still the same and he appreciated the views more, now that he was more mature. And he just liked being here by the sea, miles away from Belfast.

There were still souvenir shops and Sheila insisted on going into every one. She would have bought armfuls of brightly coloured, tacky souvenirs, which she insisted were charming, if Ray had not put his foot down. After lingering over numerous china dolls, plates with views painted on them, and even a collection of toy-size shillelaghs, she finally settled on a ceramic leprechaun with 'Souvenir of Omeath' written on it. Then before she left the shop, she bought a pair of aviator sunglasses.

'Here,' she said to Finn, 'you wear these. The girls love them.'

Feeling a little embarrassed, Finn put them on.

'They suit you,' said Ray. 'They hide that terrible squint you have!'

'Ach, very funny,' Finn replied, determined to wear the sunglasses now.

'I'm starving,' Ray announced. 'All this shopping has made me hungry.'

They made their way back down to the seafront and got three bags of chips from a van there. Only with the hot chips in his hand, did Finn realise that the day was not that warm. The unique aroma of chips covered in lashings of vinegar and salt assailed his nostrils.

'Fantastic!' he said.

'Them chips have made me thirsty,' said Ray. 'Time for a pint.'

'You're a *geg*,' said Sheila. 'Shopping makes you hungry; chips make you thirsty!'

Ray made a lunge as if to hit her but instead he put his arm round her neck and kissed her full on the lips. Finn looked away.

'Right, off to Howe's then,' said Ray.

They found a table inside the pub and Ray said, 'Three pints of Harp, is it?'

'Get me a coke,' said Finn.

'Don't you want a proper drink? I know you're underage but nobody will mind in here.'

'No, I took the pledge at my confirmation. Promised not to drink until I was twenty-one.'

'Sure, you don't even go to Mass anymore. Why would you worry about what you swore at your confirmation?'

'I took an oath,' said Finn. 'I gave my word.'

'Get him a coke for God's sake,' pleaded Sheila.

With a loud sigh, Ray went off to get the drinks.

Howe's was a traditional pub that hadn't changed at all for as long as Finn could remember. It was all dark wood panelling and brass fittings. This was the Conlyns' pub. There was another one across the way which was bigger, brighter, and more modern but they never drank there. Finn wasn't sure why. He vaguely remembered something about an argument with the landlord but didn't know the details, and even though that was years ago, when he was only a wee boy, none of the older Conlyns or Finn's generation would step one foot inside the place. The two barmen in Howe's had been there from time immemorial, that is as long as he could remember, and they never seemed to change, either in dress – clean white shirts and ties – nor age. They knew Finn and Ray by their first names and made them feel welcome.

'Is this your regular pub then, Finn? They all seem to know you here,' said Sheila.

'It's not me; it's our family. They always buy stuff in Howe's grocery shop next door and drop in here for a drink.'

Ray came back with the drinks, making a big show of giving Finn his coke. He and Sheila soon fell into banter as Finn looked on, enjoying the crack.

'This place used to be just like Killarney,' said Ray. 'You could go on a jaunting car to see all the local sights or go out to Calvary, the holy place down the road.'

'Listen to you. You're like an oul' fella. When I was a wee boy, all this was green fields,' said Sheila, in a creaky old man voice.

'I'm just saying,' said Ray.

After the second pint, Sheila had to go to the ladies. When she had gone, Ray asked, 'Are you all right, Finn?'

'Aye, I'm OK.'

'It's just you're awful quiet.'

'I'm always quiet. Sure, I can hardly get a word in with you two anyway,' he joked.

'You know you should get out of yourself more often. You know, open up a bit.' An unexpected concern entered Ray's voice, 'I know it's tough being without a da but it's been four years now. It's time you got your own life back, you know, be a bit more of a teenager.'

Finn didn't know what to say. His father's death in a stupid accident had been a blow and he still hadn't got over it. His mother took it badly and was never the same again. His younger brother and sister relied on him more than before. At the funeral his Uncle Christy had said to him, 'You're the man of the family now, son. It's up to you to look after your mammy and Brendan and Helen.' Finn had felt like a terrible burden had been placed on his shoulders. His response had been to throw himself into his schoolwork and to try to be a good son and older brother. This didn't leave much time for being a teenager.

'I'm only saying,' said Ray on seeing Finn's silence.

In a room across the hall in the pub's lounge, someone started singing. He had a good voice and soon everyone was joining in. The wave of music swept across into the bar and even Finn joined in. The songs were rebel songs and he knew the words because they were sung at all the Conlyn family gatherings: 'The Broad Black Brimmer', 'Dublin in the Green', 'Kevin Barry', and more. By the time he'd finished his third pint, Ray was getting restless. Finn knew that Ray enjoyed driving more than drinking. He loved to be behind the wheel on the open road. He was a good driver who could go fast and take bends with skill. He loved his Ford Escort which, even though it was old, he kept immaculate and was always working on, adding some accessory or fine-tuning the engine for better performance. 'Let's go,' he said, draining his glass.

Soon the car was climbing up the hill out of Omeath. Not even Ray could drive fast here. It was so steep, he had to keep in low gear, but once on top of the mountain, he could get into top gear and race along the mountain road. The mountain rose sharply on the left, and on the right there was an almost sheer drop down to the sea. Ray knew all these roads since childhood. He'd learned to drive here. With the radio blaring again the car twisted and turned along the mountain roads. Sheila held onto the door handle to steady herself but she wasn't afraid with Ray driving. They looped back by another route towards Omeath again. Then Ray pulled in off the road in a narrow glen, which the sun struggled to light up.

'We can't come up here without visiting the Long Woman's Grave. Isn't that right, Finn?'

'The what?' asked Sheila.

Ray led the way to a pile of stones nearby.

'Here it is.'

'It doesn't look like much,' Sheila commented. 'What do you mean, "Long Woman"?'

'Tell her the story, Finn.'

Finn told the story, glad of the chance to show off in front Sheila. 'Well, you know that in Irish you don't say so and so is tall. You say long. So this is the grave of the tall woman. It happened hundreds of years ago. This man O'Hanlon, one of the Irish chieftains from round here, went on an expedition to Spain. There he married a beautiful, tall woman, from one of the Irish families who had been in Spain for ages. Anyway, he brought her back here to be his lady of the manor. But while he was away, his younger brother turned Protestant and got possession of all his brother's lands. That's how it worked in those days. So when our hero and his wife came back, he found out that all his brother left him was this wee glen here, which you can see is just like being down a pit it's so narrow and high. Well, anyway, the story is that he took the Spanish lady here and told her he owned as far as the eye could see. When she looked about and saw just the sides of the glen, she dropped dead with shock and was buried there. The local people covered her grave with that pile of stones.'

'That's very sad,' said Sheila.

'Bloody eejit,' said Ray. 'Why didn't he just go back to Spain with the woman?'

They stood in silence around the grave for a while. Nothing could be heard but the sound of the wind and the occasional call of a crow or hawk. Finn thought that Sheila was saying a prayer.

'Time to head back to Belfast,' Ray announced. 'We don't want to be travelling that road in the dark.'

And so the trip to the seaside was over and they were going back to the reality of day-to-day life in Belfast. They arrived at the British army checkpoint on the Newry road pretty quickly. They all felt apprehension and were expecting some bother from the Brit who had stopped them that morning. To their relief, there was a different soldier on duty and he was happy to wave them on after a glance at Ray's driving licence. Once out of Newry, they made good speed on the road back to Belfast. They all sat in the car listening to the radio, tired and content after their day trip. Sheila started a conversation now and then, but even she was running out of energy and after a while was content to stare out of the window at the passing landscape. As they came off the M1 and drove up to the Falls Road, Ray said that he would leave Finn home first.

'But, sure, wouldn't it make more sense to drop Sheila...' he trailed off as the realisation dawned on him that the day wasn't over yet for Sheila and Ray. They wanted some time on their own. They were lucky to cross town without meeting any checkpoints and soon Ray was turning onto the Cliftonville Road.

'I'll let you out here,' Ray said at the corner of Manor Street.

'No problem,' said Finn, 'and thanks for taking me along.'

'Glad to have you, big man,' said Ray.

'Yeah, Finn, it was great that you could come along,' added Sheila. 'It was a brilliant day, wasn't it?'

Finn stood on the corner until the Ford Escort was out of sight. His holiday was over and he'd soon be back home, to his mother, to his brother and sister, to the essay that had to be finished by the following morning. It was a day in which not a lot had happened. Three friends drove to the seaside, ate ice cream, and went to a pub. They drove around and enjoyed some crack. Yet it was a day that stayed with Finn forever and one that he always remembered.

VI

What Do You Think of Ourselves?

IT WAS A SATURDAY AFTERNOON during the summer holidays and Finn was alone in the house. His mother had gone out to the park with the other two children but he did not want to go. He was hoping that Colm and Matty would call so that they could go out together, wander into the city centre or whatever. He was bored and feeling a little sorry for himself. He wished his Daddy were here. There were no boring Saturdays when he was alive. They might do something exciting like go to the seaside, or just have fun around the house, maybe a water fight in the backyard. As it was, he was sitting slouched on the sofa reading a novel, an adventure story set during World War II.

The doorbell rang unexpectedly and while Finn was speculating on who it could be, there was a violent knocking at the door. With some trepidation, Finn went out into the hall. He could make out two figures through the glass door. He knew that they were soldiers; even through the frosted glass he could see they were wearing military camouflage and that they were carrying rifles. Cautiously he opened the door a fraction and peered out at the Brits. They looked back at him with cheeky grins on their faces. From the bonnets they wore, Finn could see that they were Scottish soldiers. 'Jocks', as they called themselves.

They were young men, not much older than Finn himself. Their stockiness was exaggerated by their uniforms and they looked like hard men. The SLR rifles they carried were almost as tall as themselves. Finn guessed from their accents that they came from Glasgow, a city like Belfast that prided itself on its hard men. He never forgot his first encounter with a Scottish regiment. It was near the start of the Troubles about three years ago when the British Army had first been deployed on

the streets of Belfast and were welcomed by the Nationalist
community as a respite from the onslaught of the RUC and
Loyalists. One evening a convoy of army trucks travelled up
in Manor Street and deployed at the end of various streets
leading off it. One truck was at the bottom of Roseleigh
Street and the local children ran down to take a look at the
strangers. Finn ended up with a small group who gathered
round the tailgate of the truck. Most of the soldiers had got
out and were theatrically employed in assuming firing positions
on the street corners and nearby doorways. Two of the Jocks
remained in the back of the truck. The bolder kids asked them
were they were from. Finn interpreted the guttural response
as 'Glasgow' and a brief conversation ensued. Finn and his
friends were immediately struck by the foul language of the
soldiers. Every other word was 'fuck' or 'fucking'. Brought up
in working-class respectability and warnings from priests and
teachers about using bad language, the kids were shocked to
hear these words used so freely. It was not that they hadn't
heard them before but only when a man was angry or drunk.
Awestruck, the kids listened to the expletive-strewn dialogue
from the Jocks as they explained that they were from Glasgow,
were true-blue Prods who supported Rangers.

'Fuck Celtic!' one them shouted.

This was equally shocking to Finn and the other children
as almost everyone in the street supported that football team
and knew that their enemy, the Loyalists, supported Glasgow
Rangers. The two Jocks laughed as shock registered on the
children's faces. In a stunned silence, they turned and went
back up the street. Whose side were these soldiers on?, they
asked themselves.

The three young men eyed each other for a moment.

'Mind eff we kame in?' said the older of the soldiers.
Before Finn could answer, they both moved forward, forcing
Finn to retreat down the hall and into the sitting room. Finn
stood in the centre of the room, the Jocks in front of him.
He pointedly did not ask them to take a seat. The soldiers
unslung their rifles and propped them against their legs. They
looked around the room, paying particular attention to any

photographs or paintings that were there. Looking for clues
to political allegiance, thought Finn, but the photographs
were just pictures of his family and the two paintings were
bland landscapes that his mother liked. In other houses, Finn
knew, there would be holy pictures of Christ, the Virgin
Mary or St Patrick, often hung alongside a picture of John F
Kennedy, the only Irish-American Catholic president. Finn's
parents while devout were not ostentatious in their religion.
His mother hung her holy pictures in her bedroom.

The older Jock walked over to the bookshelf and eyed the
spines of the books. 'Ye like the reading?' he asked.

'Yes,' said Finn.

'Ye still at school?'

'Yes, I go to the local grammar school.'

'Brainy, eh?'

Finn said nothing.

'We've a few wee questions. D'ya mind?' he said as he took
a pen and a black notebook out of the pocket of his tunic,
the kind that policemen used. The other one had yet to say
a word.

'What sort of questions?' Finn asked.

'What's yer name?'

Finn told them,

'How'd ye spell that?'

It took three attempts for Finn to tell him. First, Finn's
accent was almost as indecipherable to the Jock as his was to
Finn. Then it became clear that the Scot was barely literate
and Finn had to slowly and carefully spell out his first and
last name.

'Ye live here on yer own?'

'No, with my family.'

'Who wud they be then?'

'I don't think I have to answer that,' said Finn. He had
heard of this before. A new regiment moves into a district
and they conduct a 'census' of the local population, finding
out as much as they can about who lives in a house, where
they work, what is their politics and so on. They would use
that information to profile the local population in order to

identify members of the IRA, or its political wing Sinn Féin. If someone was foolish enough to be indiscreet, Military Intelligence would use that information to blackmail them into being an informer, a tout, and they usually ended up dead. It was best not to tell the soldiers too much.

Finn and his neighbours had learned to be suspicious of the Army. It was not unusual that letters coming to the house would already be opened and clumsily resealed with sticky tape. The few people who owned phones were used to hearing whirls and clicks on the line every time they made a phonecall. They knew from spy films that this meant the line was being bugged. Finn's uncle Séan said that a few times he had even heard people with English accents speaking when he picked up the phone, clearly Brits on the line.

Finn was no hero, so he wasn't going to openly defy the soldiers or tell them to get out, but he decided he would avoid answering any more questions. When it became clear that Finn would not submit the names of his family, the one with the notebook asked,

'You got enny other family heer aboots?'

'Yes,' said Finn truthfully, 'lots. I got aunts and uncles living in this street and the next couple of streets along. And there's my cousins too.'

The soldier looked worried.

'About thirty or so,' continued Finn. 'Do you want me to give you all their names?'

The soldier with the notebook hummed and hawed. His companion smirked at his discomfort.

'You could be here a long time for me to spell out all the names,' said Finn.

'Ach, weel,' said the soldier.

'Anyway, the other soldiers will probably get their names when they call to their houses.'

A look of relief came over the soldier's face,

'Aye, maybe so,' he said. His companion's smirk grew. The soldier turned a few more pages of the notebook, then stopped and peered. Finn assumed that he must have a set of questions written there with space for the answers.

The soldier looked up at Finn. 'What'd think aboot what's gooing on?'

'Sorry,' said Finn, 'do you mean you being here in the house?'

'Nay!' the soldier seemed affronted. 'I mean aboot what's gooing on, the fightin and that.'

Finn hesitated and thought about what his reply should be. He knew that the last thing he should say was the truth. He remembered the warning about talking to the RUC or army: whatever you say, say nothing.

'I've no interest in politics,' he said, 'I just want to do my schoolwork and get my exams.'

'Oh, aye,' said the soldier. He looked at his notebook again, 'And what d'ye think of oor seff?' he asked.

Finn thought for a moment, trying to interpret what the Glaswegian had said. Was it SF? Did he want to know what Finn thought of Sinn Féin? This was dangerous ground. The wrong answer could see him hauled off to the barracks for more intensive questioning.

'Sorry?' he said.

'SF', he heard again, but then the soldier added, 'Us, the army.'

Finn breathed a sigh of relief. This was a question he could answer. 'I don't really think about you. Like I said, I've my head buried in my books.'

'Ye mean ye don't know what's gooing on?' the soldier said sceptically.

'Yes, well, I do, but I try not to get involved. I suppose you're just here doing a job. You go where you're sent.'

'Aye, right,' the soldier replied. His companion snorted.

'I've got to go out now,' said Finn. 'I've to meet my mammy in town.'

The two soldiers stared at him.

'Do youse mind leaving?' said Finn.

'Och aye,' said the older Scot. He heaved his rifle onto his soldier and made for the door. His companion made to do the same but swung his rifle as he did so that it struck Finn on the leg. It wasn't a strong blow but it hurt all the same. Finn initially flinched but was determined to show no pain.

'Ye fucking wee smart alec!' the soldier said looking Finn in the eye.

Finn did not react. The soldier followed his companion out the door.

VII

Whatever You Say, Say Nothing

INN WASN'T TOO SURPRISED that Barry should call in to say hello. As cousins they were closer than most, but he was surprised by the look on Barry's face. He was clearly worried and upset. Of all his many cousins, Barry was probably the most like Finn, even though he was a couple of years older. Like Finn, Barry enjoyed reading, always had his head stuck in a book, and was not keen on playing games, especially the rough and tumble of football on the street. Whereas Finn never got much slagging over this, Barry was the subject of barracking from both his cousins and their friends from the street. Perhaps it was that Barry exuded nervousness and when stressed spoke with a slight stammer. He should have gone to St Malachy's, like Finn, but his parents took the view that grammar school was 'not for the likes of us', and even though Barry had passed the Eleven Plus exam, he was sent to St Gabriel's, the Catholic secondary school which had a reputation for rowdiness, and found itself on the frontline when the Troubles started. It was continually under attack from stone-throwing neighbours and occasionally even gunfire. Some boys took this in their stride and even enjoyed the excitement, but it only added to Barry's state of unease and nervousness. So he was glad to quit school at sixteen the previous year. He hadn't found a job yet but he was looking for one.

So here he was, looking more worried than ever, asking to have a quiet word with Finn. Finn ushered him into the parlour. This was the room at the front of the house not used everyday by the Conlyns but kept for visitors and special occasions. Barry sat on one of the matching armchairs while Finn took a seat on the sofa. Barry hesitated to speak and Finn was aware of the noises out in the street: the yells of children playing, neighbours calling out to each other, a car engine revving...

'Well, what's up?' asked Finn.

After a false start, Barry said, 'I'm leaving, Finn. I'm getting out of here. I just wanted to tell you myself before you hear it from somebody else.'

'Leaving? Why? Where'll you go?'

'Yeah, I'm getting out of here. It's not safe for me anymore.'

'What you talking about? Not safe?' Finn looked anxiously at his cousin, trying to think of any reason he would be in danger.

'Ye remember them Brits was round last week, asking questions and that?'

'Yeah, what about them?'

'Well I just played them along, like, you know. There was two of them and they were asking me a lot of questions. You know: who lived in the house with me, did I have any relatives living in the area, did I support the IRA? That sort of thing. Well, I just bamboozled them, know what I mean. I was speaking ninety to the dozen, getting them confused with so many details and letting them get tangled up in their own questions. I know the score: whatever you say, say nothing. I never told them anything. Honest.'

'Sure I know that,' said Finn, 'so what's the problem?'

'Well after the wee Scotchies had gone, I went round to my aunt Eileen's, just to find out what the score was. She'd sent them off with a flea in their ear, just like her. So I was telling her how I'd bamboozled the Brits and told them nothing while pretending to co-operate. Sure wasn't her daughter, Sarah, there too, and that wee bitch didn't understand. She kept saying "So you told the Brits what they wanted to know?" and called me a tout.'

'That one would get you hanged,' said Finn, 'she never was too bright.'

'Aye well, I thought I'd straightened her out and thought no more about it. I thought it was a great joke the way I'd bamboozled them wee Scotchies.'

'Well, you did.'

'Aye that was alright except that the other day when I was coming out of the shop, didn't Seán Campbell pull me aside and says, "I hear you've been gabbing to the Brits." "What do you mean?" I asked him.'

Barry hesitated, his breath coming in gasps. 'Anyway he tells me that Sarah Murphy's been telling anyone who would listen that I told them Brits everything they wanted to know. It's not true, Finn! You know that!'

'Ach, Barry, you're worrying over nothing! What'd you tell Seán Campbell?'

'I said nothing! I was too scared. You know he's a Provie?'

'Well, I've heard it said that he's in the IRA, but who knows for sure?'

'The way he looked at me! I was scared shitless. I could just about say it's not true.'

Barry sat in silence, looking plaintively at Finn.

'Do you want me to talk to Seán? I was at school with his wee brother.'

'It's too late for that,' said Barry. 'I'm a marked man. You know what happens to touts.'

'Ah come on, Barry, you're worrying over nothing. People know that whatever you say, you'd say nothing to the Brits. It's just like you to worry over nothing.'

'No, Finn. I'm a marked man, thanks to that wee eejit Sarah. I'm going to England, getting out of Belfast before they come for me.'

Finn could see the panic rising in Barry. He didn't for one minute believe that the IRA were coming to get him, but no matter what he said, Barry could not be persuaded.

With a resolution that was rare in him, Barry finally announced, 'No, Finn. It doesn't matter what you say. I'm leaving. I just came to say goodbye.'

He rose to his feet and Finn stood up too. Barry held out his hand and the two cousins shook goodbye. Not another word was spoken. Barry left the house and Finn never saw him again.

Finn called round to see Barry's parents. His mother Rosie was the sister of Finn's father and they had always been close.

To Finn's surprise, she seemed quietly resigned to Barry's going.

'Ach I know why he went, Finn, and I know there was no truth in it. My Barry's no tout. That wee skitter Sarah's put the fear of God in with her loose talk. I know Seán Campbell – sure didn't I change his nappies for him when he was a wee'an? – and he's no intention of going after Barry.'

'That's what I told him,' said Finn, 'but he wouldn't listen.'

'Aye, sure I know. He took the boat across the water and he'll be in London by now, God help him.'

'Do you know where he's staying.'

'He'd no plans, and to tell the truth, I'm not sure he'll let us know.'

'You don't mean that.'

'Oh I do. Do you want to know the truth? I think he just wanted to get away. He was always an odd child and never happy. He just wanted to get away.'

Finn expected that Barry would contact his parents or even himself and say where he was in London, what he was doing.

But weeks passed and nothing came. Finn had to accept that that was it: Barry was gone for good. He was just another name on the list of people lost to the Troubles.

A Wee Hard Man

— *VIII* —

A Wee Hard Man

I T TOOK FINN A COUPLE OF MINUTES to recognise the dead RUC man. It was the main item on the news. The newsreader solemnly announced that two members of the Royal Ulster Constabulary had been killed in County Fermanagh when a bomb had exploded beside their car. There followed a few minutes of footage from the scene. An overturned car, a reinforced Ford Granada, could be seen in the background behind the reporter, wedged into the hedge at the side of a country road. RUC men and soldiers had sealed off the scene and were examining it. Then mugshots of the two constables appeared on the screen. They were head and shoulder photographs of two young men in RUC uniform, their faces partially obscured by their peaked caps. It wasn't until the name 'Kevin Myler' came on the screen beneath one of them that Finn recognised him and remembered that they knew each other.

It was about ten years ago, the summer after Finn's dad had died. It was a summer that he tried to forget. He came home from school one day to find his house full of relatives. He knew at once that something was wrong and thought of his younger brother and sister. There was no sign of Brendan or Helen, and they were usually home from school before him. His aunts were comforting his mother who sat on the sofa crying into a handkerchief.

'Come in here, Finn,' said his Uncle Christy, leading the way into the parlour at the front of the house. This room was where the best furniture was and was only used for visitors or special occasions. Uncle Christy broke the news to him gently. There'd been an accident. His Da was taken to hospital. They'd done all they could, but his Da had died.

The following weeks passed like a bad dream for Finn.

61

Uncle Christy had taken over and organised everything. None of it seemed real to Finn: not the coffin being brought to the house by solemn men dressed in black, and being set up in the parlour at the bow window; not the house being full of people day and night for what seemed like a week, sometimes talking in whispers, sometimes laughing; not the funeral Mass and the procession to Milltown Cemetery. Finn learned that his father had had a stroke while putting slates on a roof. He'd plummeted to the ground before anyone around him even knew what was happening. It seemed a senseless, stupid, death. Amidst all the violence and chaos that engulfed Belfast then, the family felt almost apologetic that Pat had died in an accident and not by a bullet or a bomb.

As the sods of earth were being thrown over his father's coffin, Uncle Christy put a comforting arm around Finn's shoulders, 'You've got to be the man of the family now, son. It's up to you to look after your mother and Brendan and Helen.'

Finn's mother was traumatised by the loss of her husband. She was in a state of shock, constantly crying, and all but ignoring her children. It was as if she was a ghost of herself haunting the house calling out for her dead husband. This was the first time that Finn learned he could forget his grief and the world around him if he submerged himself in work. He devoted his time to studying his schoolwork. He would spend much longer than was needed writing and rewriting his homework, isolated in his bedroom. He emerged only at dinner time and often had to cook for his brother and sister as his mother hardly ate and forgot to cook for them. At school, Finn's teachers noticed he was quieter than usual – he had never been outgoing – but when told about his father's death, they left him alone, apart from the priests who counselled him to pray.

Weeks became months and suddenly it was the summer holidays. Finn's mother had recovered from her grief to the extent that she was being a mother to her children again. She might have carried on in her zombie-like state except that

Finn's granny took her aside and told her she could not go on like that.

'Ach, Dear, I've lost my eldest son, but I've other childer too. And you've three wee'ans that need looking after. Do you think Patsy would want you moping about like this? He would not! Come on now. Pull yourself together and start being a mother to them childer of yours.'

The pep talk must have worked because Beth was now part of the family again, even if she was not her usual talkative, lively self. But she cooked and cleaned, and more importantly took an interest in her children and what they were up to.

Yet, a kind of stagnation affected the Conlyns. It was as if the world were in slow motion for Finn, his mother, and brother and sister. Despite the warm sunny weather, a kind of gloom hung over the house. Usually in the first few weeks after the end of school, there was talk of summer holidays and plans about where to go and what to do. There was no talk like that this year. For them all, even Helen the youngest, it seemed sacrilegious to be talking about beaches and fun and ice-cream so soon after their father's death. Finn was still disengaged to an extent, and only went through the motions of family life. Now that school was over, he could not hide from the world in books, but he could not think what to do. He began to mope around the house, which his mother said was a sin with the sun splitting the trees. His friends, Paddy and Colm, came to the rescue. They turned up on the doorstep one sunny morning and asked Finn to come to the Waterworks with them. They called every day after that and like the three musketeers they went off to do something, even if it was just mooching around the grounds of the Waterworks or window-shopping on Royal Avenue. Finn was still quiet, emotionally static, but at least he was not moping around the house.

After one of his excursions with Paddy and Colm, Finn came home to find his brother with a black eye.

'What happened to you?'

'Nothing,' was Brendan's reply.

Eventually Finn persuaded Brendan to speak. An older boy had picked on Brendan and gave him a punch. Finn loved his brother, but he knew that he had a way about him that charmed some people but infuriated others. His easy charm and quick wit sometimes had the effect of arousing hostility. Finn wasn't too surprised that some boy had turned on him; it was not the first time. But it was the first time that Brendan had been punched, and by an older boy.

'It was some fella called Kevin Myler,' Brendan finally admitted, 'but I wasn't doing nothing. Me and a couple of mates were just playing ball in the street and he showed up with some other lads. I don't know why but he just started on me for no reason.'

Finn took this final statement with some scepticism, but Brendan was his wee brother and no one had a right to hit him. He remembered Uncle Christy's words after the funeral: 'You've got to be the man of the family now, son. It's up to you to look after your mother and Brendan and Helen.' He knew he had to do something about Kevin Myler.

'Don't bother,' said Brendan. 'He's a wee hard man. He'll deck you.'

In Belfast, a hard man was someone who had a reputation not just for fighting but for being good at it. Finn had an uncle who was a hard man. A wee hard man was a teenager with a similar reputation.

Finn had no clear course of action in mind when he sought out Kevin Myler. He recalled him from his primary school. They knew each other but had never been friends. In the final year, Finn had gone into Mr O'Gorman's class and Kevin had gone into Mr Armstrong's. Kevin didn't pass the Eleven Plus and so had to go to the local secondary school, St Gabriel's. That, and the fact that Kevin lived on the Oldpark Road, meant that there had been no contact between the boys, although Finn knew of Kevin by reputation, which was being a bit of a bully and a brawler.

He found Kevin on the corner of Rosapenna Street and the Oldpark Road, where he was laying down the law to a group of boys. He didn't notice Finn approaching and looked round in surprise when Finn called out, 'Hey, Myler, I want a word with you.'

He stepped out from the rest of the boys towards Finn, hand on hips, chin out.

'What'd you want?'

'You give my brother a black eye.'

'Your brother?'

'Aye, Brendan Conlyn.'

Kevin's eyes had a distant look while he thought.

'Oh, you're Finn. The grammar school boy. Want to make something of it?'

'I'm just here to tell you to leave him alone. You lay a hand on him again and you'll pay for it.'

'What you gonna do? Recite Latin to me?'

The other boys obediently chortled at this witticism.

'You heard,' said Finn. 'Leave him alone.'

As Finn turned to walk away, Kevin called after him, 'That's it. Walk away. You're chicken, Conlyn.' He began to make clucking sounds which were taken up by the other boys.

Something came alight inside Finn. He remembered his dad and how he always told him to stand up for himself. He remembered him confronting the neighbours who hung a Union Jack outside their house the year before. His dad wasn't a hard man but he was never afraid and never ran away from a fight. He went back to Kevin, right up in his face.

'OK, put your fists up. We'll see who's chicken.'

Now Finn wasn't a fighter. He could count on the fingers of one hand the number of fights he'd been in, and none of these were serious, just scuffles in the schoolyard. But he did know something about boxing. Towards the end of his time in primary school he'd run foul of Billy, the school bully. Billy came up to him as he was leaving school one afternoon and pushed him against the wall. Billy was a stocky, tough boy who came from a family of boxers and was already a member of the parish boxing club. He pushed Finn back against the wall and delivered two expert blows to his stomach.

'That's not him, Billy,' another boy said, 'he's not the one that did it.'

Billy's fist stopped inches from Finn's nose. Without

apology, he turned round to his friend and asked, 'Who is it, then? Ye eejit.'

Finn never found out who Billy was really looking for, or what he had done to Billy's friend to earn his wrath, but when he told his dad about it that night he wasn't at all happy.

'You've got to stand up to bullies, Finn. No matter how big they are.'

Finn protested that it was all a mistake but that made no difference to his dad.

'If he comes for you again, you've got to be able to defend yourself. I'm taking you to your Uncle Oliver on Saturday.'

Uncle Oliver was the brother of Finn's Granny Conlyn. He lived on the Falls Road too but had a bigger house than his sister or anyone else in his family. He owned a small construction business and employed Finn's dad. Finn liked Uncle Oliver. He was not like any of his other old relatives in that he did not seem resigned to old age. He kept a couple of Kerry Blues, and Finn never forgot the first time he met these dogs. He was only young and the dogs almost came up to his shoulders. They were solid, muscular animals. Good fighters, his uncle said. But they were gentle with Finn and let him stroke their coats. He was immediately taken with these creatures who were at the same time strong and fierce and gentle. Uncle Oliver had been in the Old IRA and was interned in the 1950s. That made him a kind of war hero. In the IRA he'd learned a lot of things, including Jiu-jitsu, which was very exotic at the time. Not that Uncle Oliver talked about any of this: Finn learned about it from his dad.

Uncle Oliver had been a boxer in his youth and still coached young lads in his local boxing club, and that was why Finn had been brought to see him. Uncle Oliver led the way out to his backyard. Finn and his dad followed. It was a big yard with a high wall around it. Along one wall was a kennel and wired-off run for the Kerry Blues. The two dogs stood up, alert, when the three humans came into the yard. Their bright eyes were fixed on Uncle Oliver and their dark blue, almost black, coats shone in the sun. Uncle Oliver snapped an order and they lay down, quiet, keeping their gaze on their master.

Over the next hour Uncle Oliver gave Finn a few basic lessons in boxing. He showed him the right way to stand, how to make a proper fist, and how to keep his guard up.

'Keep moving your feet, Finn. Don't be a sitting target.'

Finn soon got the hang of it and in a short time, he had an experienced boxer's stance and could throw the classic combination of 'One-Two' punches. His father encouraged him and praised him when he did good, but Uncle Oliver was more critical.

'Never mind,' he said, 'I don't suppose at your age you'll come against Muhammad Ali.'

Finn was brought a couple of more times to get lessons from his great uncle, but then it stopped. Uncle Oliver said there was no point in doing any more unless Finn was going to take up boxing seriously. Patsy, his father, was in favour of this, but Finn was not enthusiastic and his mother was dead set against it. However, he did keep on practising and, even if he never fought anyone, he still had the moves.

Kevin Myler was a big boy for his age. He looked more fifteen than thirteen. He was broad shouldered and muscular. As Finn stood in front of him, he had an overwhelming sensation of Kevin's solidity. It was like he was made of concrete. In contrast, Finn felt weak in front of Kevin and a feeling came over him like he was fading away, that his own solidity was dissolving. For a fleeting second, he thought about turning tail and running away. Instead, he assumed the boxer's stance, his fists held close in front of him.

'Hey, this isn't fair,' Kevin called out, a slight tremor in his voice, 'he's a trained boxer. I'm not.'

'You want to chicken out?' said Finn.

Kevin hesitated, but the other boys began to make clucking sounds, creating a chorus of derision.

Kevin charged forward. Finn easily sidestepped him but his first punch failed to connect. Kevin came at him again, not charging this time, but steadily approaching his opponent. Finn realised that Kevin was not trained to fight. He'd been used to using his height and weight against his opponents, mostly boys his own age or younger. That's what his hard man reputation was built on. He swung a haymaker at Finn, who ducked under his arm and landed a one-two on Kevin's stomach. He was solid and Finn's punches made little impact. He came at Finn again, swinging both his large fists. Finn danced in front of him, still nervous about Kevin landing a punch. The group of boys were enjoying the fight, cheering for Kevin or Finn. One even started up a commentary, imitating Harry Carpenter, famous for commenting on Muhammad Ali's fights for the BBC. Kevin kept swinging at Finn and Finn kept dancing out of reach, landing punches that seemed to have no effect on Kevin. Then Finn parried a right hook from Kevin and directed a punch with his right fist onto Kevin's kidney, as hard as he could. The bigger boy flinched at this and dropped his guard. Finn got in two jabs with his left hand on Kevin's jaw. Finn could feel a sharp pain run up his arm from his fingers to his shoulder, but Kevin staggered back, his hands going to his face.

'This isn't fair,' he cried, 'Finn's a boxer. I'm not.'

'Are you throwing in the towel?' Harry Carpenter asked.

'Yeah, I am,' said Kevin, holding back tears.

Finn did not feel elated at his victory. After all, it seemed a small thing compared to his dad's death. He'd done his duty by Brendan. That was all. He stood there in silence as Kevin and a few loyal followers retreated up the Oldpark Road. The other boys gathered round Finn congratulating him and complimenting his boxing skills.

'I'm going back home now,' he said and walked away, nursing his left hand.

One outcome of the fight was that Finn now had a reputation that he was someone who could look after himself, and that protection extended to Brendan. The other outcome was that Kevin had respect for Finn and even tried to make friends with him. It didn't matter much to Finn. He and Kevin led very different lives: Finn devoted himself to doing well at school and did not hang about in the streets much, except during the summer holidays. His and Kevin's paths did not cross often. A few years after their fight, Kevin's family moved out of the Oldpark Road. Finn didn't know exactly where they moved to but someone said it was into one of the new housing estates in Glengormley to the north of the city.

Now, seeing his photograph on the television, Finn wondered why Kevin had joined the RUC. It was always seen as a Protestant force that did not welcome Catholics. There had been some reforms in the early years of the Troubles but to Finn and most of the people he knew the RUC was still an enemy force: ninety per cent Protestant, one hundred per cent Unionist, as a slogan painted on a wall on the Falls Road put it. Kevin must have known what he was getting into. The RUC didn't carry guns for no reason. They had killed people, co-operated with Loyalist gangs in the random assassination of Catholics, and Castlereagh RUC Station was notorious for how prisoners were treated there. Kevin was built for an RUC man, thought Finn. They all seemed to be bulky six-footers. Maybe he liked the idea of a uniform and a gun. Finn didn't think that Myler had joined the RUC out of a sense of idealism. He knew of one Catholic, the older brother of a boy he'd been at St Malachy's College with, who believed that if enough Catholics joined they could change the RUC for the better.

Automatically, Finn added Kevin Myler to the mental list of people he knew who had died in the Troubles: Uncle Christy, Uncle Jimmy, Terry Morgan, other neighbours from home. Kevin's death didn't seem exceptional. Once, when he'd been drinking in the Bot with Paddy and Colm, another ex-pupil of Sacred Heart Primary School showed up out of the blue. They hadn't seen Aidan for years. He didn't pass the Eleven Plus and he left St Gabriel's at the first chance he got. He'd been living in England for a while and seemed to be doing alright for himself, something unspecified in the music business. He insisted on buying them a drink and as he sat down with them, he began to reminisce about their childhood, asking after this boy or that. As they filled in the blanks – Paddy and Colm were much better at keeping track of people than Finn was – it became clear that of the forty-two boys in their year, only about half had ordinary lives. Some had just dropped off the radar, the rest were in prison, on the run, or dead. So there was nothing special about Kevin.

Yet, Finn felt sorry for him. He'd been a part of his life, and if not exactly friends there had been an understanding between them. However he died, it was a waste that Kevin was killed so young. He was another victim, another life thrown away because of the Troubles. He remembered him as a boy, a wee hard man, but still a boy. And now he would never marry, never have children, never grow old.

Finn had to admit to himself that if it had been someone else from his old primary school, no matter how slightly he knew him, he would attend the funeral, but Kevin Myler's was one funeral that Finn would not be attending.

IX

Haunted

SUMMER CAN BE a lonely, boring time for a shy, bookish boy. An only child of ageing parents, he had never got used to the rough and tumble of play with other boys, never took to the jostle and barging of football or other games, and never felt at ease with the banter that teenage boys exchanged. Most of the summer he wished for school, for the anonymity of a crowd, of the refuge of burying his head in a book at his desk, and using homework as an excuse not to have to go out to play as his parents coaxed him. He did not mind the days that it rained, for then he could stay in his room and read. The bike he got the Christmas before proved a godsend as he could take it out on the dry days when his mother was at him to go out and get some fresh air and sunshine.

He enjoyed the solitude of cycling through the country roads that radiated from the village. He liked experiencing the sights and sounds of rural life: the sheep and cows in the fields, the birdsong and even the occasional chat with an old bachelor farmer who would not let him pass without giving him the time of day.

He was out on one of these rides when his stomach told him that it was getting late and he had better go home. He rode down one road, and then turned onto another that led home, when a dark, mud-spattered van with two men in it came along the middle of the road in his direction. As it neared, the passenger in the van rolled down the window and signalled for him to stop.

'You can't go down here, son. The road's closed. You'll have to go the other way round,' he said in a flat voice.

As he watched the van drive off, he considered his options. If he did not take this road, the alternative route would add another couple of miles onto his journey. He was in no mood to cycle that extra distance and it would make him late. Besides he felt a certain resentment at being curtly told that he could not go on down this road, a road he had cycled hundreds of times. Mounting his bike, he set off down the road.

He was just turning the first bend when he saw the car. It was parked at an awkward angle, nose in towards the ditch. Instinctively he stopped, and, one foot resting on the ground, watched. A man wearing a dark khaki jacket and carrying some black object in his hand was opening a rear door. Another man got out and stood there. A third man got out of the driver's side and walked swiftly round the car to where the others were. The three moved towards a gate in the hedge.

He could see that the man in the middle was being forced by the other two but he offered no resistance. He was dishevelled, unshaven, and had a beaten look about him. The boy knew immediately what was going on. The men had taken no notice of him yet, and he looked about him for somewhere to get out of sight. On the other side of the road a half-open, rusty gate led into a field to a couple of dilapidated sheds. Dismounting he went as quietly as he could into the field. He wheeled his bike along the hedge and propped it up there. He hunkered down, pushing himself in against the hedge even though the thorns stung his back, hoping that this would make him invisible.

He sat and waited. Nothing happened. Then a beetle appeared on the back of his right hand and began to crawl slowly up his arm. It was black, shiny, and moving very slowly, carefully negotiating the hairs on his arm. He watched it and waited. Time crawled as slowly as the beetle. He wondered why it was taking so long. Maybe they were giving him a chance to say his prayers.

Just as the beetle reached the rolled-up sleeve of his shirt he heard the shot. A sharp, explosion that disturbed the silence and made the birds take to the air cawing and shrieking. He pushed himself further into the hedge. A few minutes later he heard car doors opening and closing. Then the car drove past him, the gears wrenching as it speeded up. Still he did not move.

When he was sure that the men in the car had gone, he brought his bike back to the road and got on. He wanted to cycle fast but could not. As he passed the open gate, he dared take a glance into the field. He could make out a dark shape just out of sight, only mud-spattered trousers and bruised bare feet showed.

The next day the whole village was abuzz with the story. He and his school friends talked about the body that had been found, and soon it was established that the dead man was a tout, a police informer. It was because of him that the Brits had wiped out that Active Service Unit six months ago. There was no sympathy expressed for the dead man and he did not feel any for him either.

It was something of a ritual for him and his parents to sit with their dinners on their laps, his dad on his armchair, he and his mother on the sofa, and watch the teatime news. That was where he saw the funeral. His mother said a brief prayer for the dead man and uttered words of sympathy for his wife and children. He should have thought of them before he turned tout, was his father's opinion. He watched the funeral unmoved, until they showed the widow and her four children at the graveside. The camera narrowed in on the eldest, a girl of about his own age, who was crying like he had never seen anyone cry before. It caused him pain just to see the tortured look on her face and hear her say in a plaintive voice, 'Daddy. Daddy.'

He did not sleep well that night or any night after. It was not that he had nightmares or flashbacks. He just felt a great sadness and could not settle. His mother noticed the change in him but thought it was because he was going back to school in a couple of weeks after the long summer break. At school he began to falter. Once the teachers thought him the brightest in his class and even spoke optimistically of him going on to university, a rarity in this part of South Armagh. Now he did not pay attention in class and was too often caught daydreaming when asked a question by a teacher. His homework was just adequate and he scraped through the end-of-year exams. His teachers put it down to his age. As boys get older they have other interests and schoolwork drops off their agenda, they said to each other.

And so it went on. He just lived, got through his daily life by following the path of least resistance. He came home, did his homework, and sat in front of the television. If his mother told him to go out and play he did that but with no enthusiasm. With the passing of the days, weeks, and then months, he thought less and less about that day and the girl on TV. Eventually it was out of his mind completely and he could not think why life had lost its lustre or why he could never sleep properly.

But there was always a presence. That was how he came to think of it. Something was shadowing him. There were times when he thought that if he could just turn round quick enough he would see it; but he never did. The presence was always with him. It would squeeze itself onto the sofa between him and his mother. At school he knew it was standing just behind his desk or sometimes hovering above his head. When he lay in bed at night, it stood there in the darkness beside the bed looking down at him.

He passed his O-levels with average grades. The talk of going on to A-levels and university had long since sunk without trace. It did not matter to his parents who had both left school at fourteen and for whom university was not even a faraway dream. After a while he got a clerical job in a department store in Newry. Every day he travelled in on the bus, and every night he travelled home. Using the excuse that he was tired, he went to his bedroom after dinner and lay on the bed staring at the ceiling, the presence standing guard over him.

The people in work said that he was alright but a bit too shy. He did not join in with the chitchat, jokes, and gossip that oil relations in any office. Even though his workmates coaxed him he would never go for a drink after work or with them to watch a football match at the weekends. Yet no one could complain. He was neat, tidy, did his work and caused no trouble.

This continued for two years and then he got a flat in the town. An overheard casual reference made him realise that he could move away from home into his own place. His parents acquiesced hoping that it would make him happy and that he was moving to be closer to a girlfriend. He liked living on his own except for the presence. It still shadowed him everywhere he went. He would feel it hovering near his desk at work and following him up the street when he was out. No matter what room he went to in his flat, it was there, silent and watchful.

Then he found that he could forget about it if he drank enough. Alcohol had never been a part of his life but he saw people drunk and they seemed happy for the most part. He tried drinking in the local pub but got uncomfortable when someone engaged him in conversation. He did not want to tell anyone where he was from, what he worked at, and why he had no girlfriend; and he did not care to find out about other people. So he took to buying beer in an off-licence and was content to sit in his flat and drink it while watching television. He was still aware of the presence but drink seemed to dull his perception and the presence sometimes faded so much that he almost forgot it was even there.

But some summer evenings, when the sun cast long shadows on the mountains, he would remember his days of cycling along the roads back home. Then the presence would be stronger and after a few drinks he found himself talking to it. He would ask why was it there; plead with it to leave him; and often end up shouting and cursing at it. He would fall into bed in a drunken sleep and wake up in the morning feeling hungover and sick, to find the presence standing by his bed.

One day someone made a joke in work at his expense and he left. His boss tried to talk him out of it but he was having none of it and quit. He found it hard to get another job and so signed on the dole. He had no worries or responsibilities. He signed on once a fortnight, and with his cheque bought enough food and drink to keep him going. This was alright for a while, but soon it began to wear thin. He discovered that he needed work and the distraction of other people. The days dragged slowly by. The presence was always there and he could not ignore it. Sometimes he found it a struggle to get through just one minute at a time. He blamed Newry and called it a lousy town where there was no work and nothing to do. He decided to move to Belfast, and found it surprisingly easy to transfer to the unemployment office there and get a cheap flat in the north of the city.

For the first few days he was happy. He had never been to Belfast before and he enjoyed exploring it, at least those areas where it was safe for a stranger to go. He was settling in to his flat – three rooms in a large Victorian terrace house. It was not until the presence returned that he realised that it had been gone. He was no longer alone and his brief happiness evaporated. The presence was there again. He felt it alongside him when he queued to sign on every fortnight. It insinuated itself between him and other people on a crowded bus going into the city centre. It followed him everywhere he went in the flat, just like it had always done at home and in Newry.

Eventually he got a job as a security guard in a large store in the city centre. Everywhere had guards who searched handbags and kept an eye out for suspicious people in case someone was trying to plant a bomb. It was an unpopular job and there were always vacancies. He was glad to get it even though it paid just a little more than he got on the dole.

It was a job that suited him. He was not required to mix with the other security men. They seemed similar to him in some ways. When they happened to be in the same room together at tea-break or lunchtime, there was little or no conversation. They all behaved like men who feared revealing personal information or giving anything away. And that suited him. The days passed easily enough, and over the months he became known to regular customers. Some would give him a 'Good day' and make some comment about the weather, and he was happy enough to reply in kind. The work could be tiring though, and it would not take many drinks to send him off to sleep at night.

The presence was still there. At quiet times in the store, as he stood watching the shoppers scuttle back and forth on the street outside through the big plate-glass doors, he would feel it just behind him. Sometimes even when he was busy, like on a Saturday morning when he was continually looking into handbags or patting down customers, he would feel it there, near him, lurking just behind the next customer, ever present but out of sight. At night too when he got home exhausted and tried to lose himself in television or drink, he would know that it was there. But he was resigned to it now and barely recalled a time when the presence was not near.

Then one day it happened. He recognised her instantly as she came in through the doors. She went to the security man next to him to have her handbag checked. He looked at her. She was ten years older but still pretty. To his surprise she bore no marks of her tragedy. He expected her to look sad, to look as though she was suffering with dignity, but she looked like any other young woman out for a day's shopping – except that she was on her own.

It all came back to him, taking his breath away, sucking the blood from his heart. He saw himself riding his bicycle down the quiet road on that sunny evening. He remembered the car and the men; him, a frightened little boy, hiding behind the hedge; the beetle crawling up his arm. Everything came back to him.

He left his post and followed her into the shop heedless of the man who stood before him waiting to be searched and the exclamation of the security man on the other door. He followed her from a distance as she strolled through the store looking at this dress or that, taking a blouse off a rail to try it against her and checking prices on cardigans. She seemed to have no purpose in her wandering and soon she left the store, this time by the back door. This led out onto a quiet street that ran parallel to Royal Avenue. There were not many shops left in it and so fewer people about.

He stepped quickly out after her and caught her arm. She looked around, startled. She saw his uniform and was frightened. He began to speak in breathless, hurried sentences.

He explained that he knew who she was. He told her how he had been there when her father was killed and that he had seen her on the TV.

She said nothing. She looked at him, and their eyes were locked for what seemed like minutes. Time crawled past slowly like the beetle crawled along his arm.

She took a step back, recoiling from his presence, and then she spoke, 'You were there and did nothing?'

'I was only a wee boy,' he said weakly.

She slapped his face. Hard. It shocked him and hurt, but he said nothing, did nothing. He had not thought when he followed. Had not thought how she would react. Had he expected gratitude? She turned her back to him and hurried away. He just stood there watching her retreating out of view. And for the first time in ten years he was utterly alone. The spell was broken: the presence gone.

X

Escape

FINN HAD BEEN WORKING LATE in the university library. He had a fifteen-hundred-word term paper to finish and had got caught up in chasing down information and references. It wasn't that the paper was due soon, but once he started working on it, he was carried along in the pursuit of knowledge. He wanted to find a new angle to approach the topic. He was into his second year at Queen's University and was really enjoying his time. It was like being part of the adult world but without the responsibilities of an adult. For the first time in his life, he had his own money, thanks to the student grant, and the university gave him an alternative focus to the streets of North Belfast that had compassed his existence for so long. He liked the fact that he had lectures and tutorials in a timetable that left much of the day free, and he accepted that it was his responsibility to learn and produce work. Some of the other first years had found it hard to adapt.

Most of all, he loved that his horizons had been widened. For the first time in his life, he had become friends with Protestants. The university, if not exactly a neutral zone, was somewhere where you could find out about another person's religion and politics without resorting to shouting, and certainly without violence. Some of his early encounters with Protestants were odd to say the least. He had not been at the university long when he found himself alone in the departmental common room with a Protestant boy, whose people owned a big farm near Ballymena. They started to chat and Finn was taken aback when he asked, 'Do Catholics still eat babies at Mass?' Finn explained what Mass was about, when the boy came back with, 'And the nuns. Are they there to have sex with the priests?' Patiently Finn explained that this was not so. Later he wondered if the Protestant lad hadn't been pulling his leg.

Northern Ireland might been going up in flames around them but most of the staff and students discussed the events and their causes as if they were merely intellectual issues. Finn was also introduced to international politics and learned about the Cold War, apartheid in South Africa, and the State of Israel. He was given a much wider perspective on the world. Within the Students' Union, things were more serious. The various parts of the political spectrum were represented by different societies, and arguments between them could get heated, but Finn was not interested in any of this. The murder of Uncle Christy the year before had been a living nightmare for him and he had not recovered from it yet. He couldn't get out of his mind taking the phone call to hear that Christy was shot, nor seeing his mother collapse onto a sofa when he told her. And he could still feel the agony of phoning his aunt to tell her that Christy had died. In his sleep, he saw his uncles and friends of Christy wipe away their tears at his funeral, and hear the crying of his wife and sisters as the coffin was taken from the house. Being at university was an escape from North Belfast: he was happy to lose himself in his studies and would spend hours in the library reading books.

There were three friends who'd come up from St Malachy's College with him, and although they were doing different degrees, they still hung out together. To these were added other friends, Catholic and Protestant, who all together formed a group that met up at lunchtime and went drinking together in the evening. He had discovered that drink helped. For a few hours drinking with his mates in the students' union bar, he could lose himself in the academic arguments they had, or in swapping funny stories and jokes; and he found too that he could sleep without dreams if he went to bed drunk. He usually left in time to catch an early bus home – he wasn't the only one – but occasionally he might end up sleeping on the floor of someone's flat. It was never safe to travel the city late at night, but sometimes he did.

Tonight was one of those nights, and he had an uneasy feeling as he sat on the late bus going from the city centre to the Cliftonville Road. The Troubles had heightened a latent fear of being attacked. He could remember the first time that he was beaten up for being a 'Fenian bastard.' He was only seven at the time and had been more shocked that the two boys, about ten or eleven years old, had used the word bastard. He wasn't badly hurt as they only gave him a couple of punches and then ran off. That was not the last occasion that he happened to be in the wrong place at the wrong time. Once the wrong place was just a couple of streets away from his home. His was a mixed area where Catholic and Protestant lived relatively peacefully and so his guard was down when he turned the corner and ran into four boys, teenagers like himself. If he had known who they were there, he would have given them a wide berth, but he walked right into them, and knew he was in trouble. He was on his way home from school and one of them spotted his school tie. 'A Taig!' he cried to his companions, and Finn was suddenly cowering under a shower of fists and feet. He managed to curl up against a wall, leaving himself only partly exposed but his legs and arms were covered in bruises, and his nose bleeding, when they finished.

He had even more reason to be concerned now. His bus would stop just above Manor Street and he had a five-minute walk home from there. Last summer a man from the area was found dead on this corner, near the sweet shop that Finn loved when he was younger, beaten and chopped up with a hatchet. The Shankill Butchers were blamed for the murder. This loyalist gang was notorious for randomly kidnapping, torturing, and murdering Catholics. Their victims were beaten and cut up with a butcher's knife or a hatchet. Other Catholics had been shot at and killed by a passing car while walking along the Cliftonville Road. It was said that the UVF had sent out fliers to Protestant houses warning them not to walk on the left side of the road so that they would be sure of killing only Taigs.

Finn looked anxiously around as the bus approached his stop, looking for a suspicious car or a group of men who didn't belong. As the bus got nearer the stop, he realised that there was some activity on the corner of Manor Street. There were grey RUC Land Rovers and green British Army Land Rovers parked there, while RUC men and soldiers milled about. 'It's a raid,' thought Finn. He dreaded getting off the bus as he might end up against the wall being questioned by the RUC, having them go through all the books in his bag, or worse, being lifted and brought to a barracks. He contemplated waiting to get off at the next stop further up the road but that would mean a longer walk through dark streets to get home.

He got off the bus and walked down towards Manor Street. There were a number of local people watching what was going on. Finn had never seen anything like this before. Neither the RUC nor the soldiers seemed interested in the locals. They were walking around, some with torches, examining the ground. At one spot, an RUC man was kneeling down peering at the pavement, while another one took photographs, his camera's flash momentarily bathing everyone in lightning every time he took a photo. Finn recognised someone from his own street.

'What's going on, Mrs Morgan?'

'Ah, Finn, you were lucky you weren't here half an hour ago.'

'Why? What happened?'

'Them Shankill Butchers tried to lift a young fella off the street. He was just coming up the road when a car pulled in beside him. Two fellas got out and tried to grab a hold of him. He was too quick for them and they missed him, but they came after him and one of them hit him with a hatchet. He fought back and they got a few more swipes at him. Luckily someone heard the commotion and came out onto the street. Well, they raised a racket when they saw what was happening and the Butchers jumped back into their car and took off.'

'Is the man dead?' Finn asked.

'No, he's in the Mater. We don't know if he'll live or not. Lord have mercy.'

When he got home, his mother was standing in the hall waiting for him.

'Thank God and His blessed mother, you're home safe!' she said. 'Did you hear what happened? A young fella was attacked on Manor Street. I was worried sick it was you.'

'I know. There's still Brits and RUC men there. I'm alright. Don't be worrying.'

'Don't be worrying? That could have been you! I worry about you coming home at night. Anybody could lift you off the street.'

'I'm not always on my own,' he said, 'Usually Paddy or Colm is with me.'

'Aye, but they live on up the road. They don't walk up Manor Street with you.'

'I know, mammy. I do be careful.'

'Do you want any supper?' she asked.

'No, I'll just watch some TV and then go to bed. It's late enough and I've a nine o'clock lecture in the morning.'

The next morning, as he had ate his bowl of cereal in the kitchen, Finn's mam turned from washing the dishes to say, 'You know, son, I've been thinking. Would it not be better for you to live over at the university?'

'I hadn't thought about it. It would cost money.'

'Don't they have halls of residence that are cheap enough?' she said, 'I was taking to Annie Monaghan, and her son's at Queen's now. He lives in the halls of residence. She says he gets a grant on account he comes from a deprived area. Sure, you could do that.'

Finn was surprised. His mother had always been protective of him since his father had died when he was just a boy, and wanted to keep him close.

'But I wouldn't want to leave you and Brendan and Helen here on your own. It wouldn't be right.'

'Ach, we'll be fine. Sure Brendan's nearly a man now himself. And we'll be a lot safer here than you, traipsing across town and back going to university. After what happened last night, I'm heart scared that you'll end up chopped to bits and dumped on the street.'

'Don't be saying that, mammy.'

'No, I'm serious. I'd be happier knowing you were living over there and safe.'

'Well, OK. I'll look into it,' he said.

In fact, Finn had been thinking about moving to the university area for a while. Not only did he worry about travelling across the city, but he felt he was wasting time doing it. He would not have to worry about staying too late at the library, or turn down invitations to parties or gigs if he had his own place to walk home to. He stayed on at home because he felt bad about abandoning his family. Admittedly since the Peace Wall had been built between them and the River Streets, there had been no Loyalist mobs trying to burn them out, but there were other threats. He knew that he was in danger every time he walked on the Cliftonville Road or Manor Street after dark. His mother was right: he would be safer staying close to the university. Besides he could still come home to visit. Queen's was not a million miles away.

It didn't take many weeks to get a room in the student accommodation and, to his surprise, the Education Authority even gave him a grant to cover the rent. Soon, Finn had settled into life as a full-time student. He was no longer worried about going home after dark, and he could stay out as late as he liked. For the first time in his life, he ate Chinese, Italian, and even French food, as there were a variety of restaurants on University Road and Botanic Avenue. He got to go to concerts as many bands came to perform at Queen's, even some big acts from Britain. And he got to know girls. He still struggled with shyness and didn't want to tell anyone about the tragedies in his family, which made things awkward, but he made friends with girls and slowly his lack of confidence began to fade. In this part of the city he was free of all the concerns and worries that had weighed him down while he lived in North Belfast. There were times when he even forgot that the Troubles were happening, and the terrible things that happened to his family.

He felt that he was two different people. One Finn was the Catholic boy from North Belfast and the other was Finn the university student. When he was back home, he didn't tell family or friends too much about his life at Queen's. His mother was a Pioneer of Total Abstinence and would have been shocked at how much he drank on a night out. To his aunts and uncles, the university was an alien world and they didn't show much interest in the intricacies of balancing a lecture timetable, or the differences between romantic and modern poetry. At university, many of his friends wouldn't have believed, never mind understood, the sort of community he came from. The Protestants from middle-class homes in particular couldn't understand why anyone wanted to be Irish and didn't trust the security forces. Finn couldn't tell them about the hurt of having someone close to you murdered or the fears of attack in your own home. He found it easier to develop a different persona, that of a happy student, lost in his studies and enjoying the social life that Queen's had to offer.

However, he could not escape the Troubles entirely. There was an Ulster Defence Regiment base on the Malone Road and he would often see their Land Rovers driving through the university district. They were locally recruited Protestants, and he didn't want to be stopped by them. There were stories that they give Catholic students a hard time. Colm told of the night that he had been walking up the Malone Road with his new best mate, Adam. They'd had a few drinks in the Students' Union and were on the way back to the halls of residence. They must have seemed too lively, for a passing UDR jeep suddenly stopped and the soldiers jumped out. They put the students up against the wall and asked them for ID. The demeanour of the UDR men, middle-aged men from the country, was openly hostile and suspicious. The corporal in charge closely examined their student identity cards and asked them questions about where they 'really lived' when they gave their address as the halls of residence. He went back to the Land Rover and was on the radio for a few minutes. All the while other students went past, looking curiously at what was going on. The corporal called Adam over to him and asked him to stand behind the jeep.

'Do you realise, wee fella, that the person with you is a Catholic?'

'Yes,' said Adam, 'He's my best mate. We share a room together.'

'Are you kidding me, son?' the corporal said in amazement.

'No, honest, he's my friend,' said Adam, wondering what the problem was.

'Well,' said the UDR man, 'I'll tell you something. You're lucky it was us that stopped you. If another patrol found out you were best friends with a Fenian, you'd be in big trouble. Know what I mean?'

Adam wasn't going to argue the point. Only when the UDR jeep was well away from them, did he explain to Colm what had happened.

And Finn could not forget the ties of family. He made sure that he went back home at least once a week to see his mother and check up on his brother and sister; usually he went for Sunday dinner which was also the chance to get a proper meal.

And then one morning, before eight o'clock, someone hammered on his room door. 'There's someone on the phone for you.'

Pulling on some clothes, Finn took the lift down to the reception area of the hall of residence. There was a row of phone booths against one wall. Another student he knew by sight said into one of the phones, 'He's here now.'

With trepidation, Finn lifted the receiver to his ear.

'Is that you, Finn?' he heard his mother's voice.

'Yes, Mammy, it's me.'

'Finn. You've got to come home. Your Uncle Jimmy's been shot.'

XI

Damaged

H E STILL HAD NIGHTMARES even though he had been on the outside now for over ten years. He thought of them as nightmares but they were not dreams, more like the memories of something he did not want to remember. He would wake up in the dark, afraid and uncertain. He was gripped by a feeling that something was wrong and that he could not fix it. He would lie as still and silent as he could in the bed for fear of waking his wife up. He knew that if this happened she would try to comfort and reassure him, but it would be hollow for she did not understand his terror. She did not know the right words. She had never been inside Long Kesh.

He told himself that he had only four more years to go and then it would be over. He had been inside for fourteen years and it would take fourteen years on the outside before he would be normal. That seemed rational to him. It would take the same number of years on the outside as he had spent in the prison in order for that experience to work itself through his system. So fourteen years inside meant he had to spend fourteen outside in order to be cured. He could put up with it for four more years. That was the certainty that kept him going. He had been able to resist the temptation to get lost in drink or drugs because of that certainty. He knew some of his comrades who had gone over to the dissidents because a life undercover and on the run was easier to cope with than a normal life. He did not want that. His certainty that his personal hell would all end in four years kept him sane.

He had joined the organisation when just a teenager. His family were not political and tried their best to ignore the Troubles, but he could not ignore what he saw on TV and what he experienced on the streets. The constant sight of

British Army patrols was bad enough but the being stopped and questioned, put up against a wall and searched really made him angry. There was no one thing that made him decide to join up. He had been arrested once and held overnight in the barracks because the mate he was with could not keep his mouth shut. The silly bugger had to curse and swear at the Brits who held them against the wall while they went through their pockets. He did not react right away when a neighbour was gunned down on his doorstep by Loyalists, but eventually he came to the conclusion that he had to fight back. He would not be a man otherwise.

It was not straightforward joining up. Making contact with a known Provie was easy but convincing them that he was serious, and could take it, was a lot harder. It was months before he was accepted and allowed to swear the oath to the Republic. He had no idea about what he would do inside the IRA. He had a vague notion of gunfights or sniper ambushes. An idea of striking back at the Brits, the RUC, and the Loyalists, but that was all. Despite being bright enough, he had not been good at much at school except at chemistry and physics.

They put him to making bombs.

That was nerve-wracking work. Homemade explosives and jury-rigged timing devices were dangerous in themselves even before you put them together for a bomb. He was always worried that the bomb might go off early and kill him or the unit planting it. He stopped watching the news on television. He did not want to see what his handiwork had achieved, or to hear from the TV that a comrade had been killed because a device he had put together had gone off prematurely. It was almost a relief when a joint army and RUC patrol broke down the front door in the early hours of the morning. The Brits charged in shouting at the top of their lungs and pointed their rifles at his head. An RUC man solemnly stood at the foot of the bed and told him he was being arrested. He went without resistance: he was glad it was over.

Someone – he never found out who – had talked under a brutal interrogation, and given them his name. They found some stuff in the house, not much, just a timer and wiring.

He knew he was stupid to take it home. Months on remand were followed by a quick trial and a sentence to life in prison. He bore no ill will towards the guy who had talked. He was not sure that he would have done different. And now the uncertainty, the fear, had been taken out of his life. He had no more worries about his bombs going off prematurely or waiting to be arrested. In prison, awaiting trial, every minute of his time was regulated. Long Kesh was the same. He was drafted into the organisation in there, assigned a role in the hut he was put into.

Many of his comrades took advantage of the educational opportunities offered and studied for degrees with the Open University, but that was not for him. He learned to play the guitar. He was happy to go along with all the activities and protests that the boys in command organised. If that were all, he could have survived intact, but the struggle was carried on inside the prison. There were protests, refusal to wear prison uniform, and the Hunger Strikes. He wasn't called on to go on the strike but he participated in disrupting the prison along with the other prisoners. The screws reacted to all this by laying on the violence. Every way to humiliate the men was put into effect, and then randomly someone would be picked out for a beating. The whole experience left him shattered, and now he tried to wipe the experience from his mind.

After he got out because of the Good Friday Agreement, he could not adjust to life on the outside. He had not finished his education, had no skills and no trade except that of bomb-maker. He drifted down to Dundalk, south of the Border, where he stayed a year and learned to tend bar. After that he went to the United States, spent time there as an 'illegal', and then he went on to France where he found work in Irish bars in Paris and Marseilles. But he never settled. He made no close friends and was never in any one place long enough to call it home. He came back to North Belfast, to his old neighbourhood, his family, and childhood friends. He met Margaret, whom he knew as a wee girl from up the street. She was now an attractive woman and she liked him. He supposed he fell in love with her. She fell for him, the man who had been inside, who had suffered for the Cause. Getting married was the natural thing. He never proposed, but an unspoken agreement was reached and a day set. Marriage gave him an anchor and a stability that he had not had up until then. He found out that married life was a routine just like the Kesh had been a routine.

He tried not to think about his time in the Kesh. A lot of the boys did nothing else. They spent their days sitting together in this social club or that, talking about their years in the cages or the H-Blocks. Their stories usually ended in forced laughter or sometimes in tears. He preferred to sit with those who did not recount those years. He would talk of anything but what had happened there.

He went to the club twice a week. That was part of his routine. Once on a Friday night to drink by himself, and then on Saturday him and the wife went together because a band was playing. The routine was important to him. It ruled his life. His old OC, now a community worker, had got him a part-time job in a social centre. Three afternoons a week he went there. He was the only one that never took time off and he always went on holiday the same fortnight every year. People would sometimes joke about it, and he joked along. He could never admit to them that he needed this certainty in his life. He needed to know that when he woke up on Tuesday morning, say, he would be going down to work in the centre that afternoon, and that at half-five he would come home again.

The certainty kept him sane. It had begun in a general way: the reassurance of his weekly routine, knowing where he would be on any given day of the week. But the longer he was on the outside, the more detailed it became. He had to know that he would have the same breakfast every morning. He knew just what was for dinner every night of the week. He and Margaret sat down to watch television at the same time every night and always watched the same programmes. That was the only way in which he felt in control; the only way to keep a breakdown at bay.

One night he came in from the centre, grateful to have got through another day in which nothing unexpected or out of the ordinary happened. He was looking forward to his supper.

His wife was in the kitchen. He sat on the living-room sofa watching TV and they talked to each other through the open door in the way that settled couples do. After a while she called him into the kitchen to get his supper. He stared down at the table. A grilled chicken breast lay on his plate. It was supposed to be a pork chop tonight. He turned on her, demanding to know why she had betrayed him. Couldn't she remember a simple thing like buying pork chops? Did she really hate him that much?

Her explanations about running late and finding the butcher sold out of chops went past his ears. The floor beneath his feet turned to sand. The solid walls around him melted away. He was overwhelmed by terror. He was being sucked back in there and it was her fault. Had she no idea how fragile this all was? Could she not see that if everything wasn't just right, it would all fall apart?

He did not remember what happened her. He was suddenly aware that she was hanging onto the edge of the sink, her face bruised, sobbing but determined not to scream out her pain. He stared down at her in silence before running from the kitchen. In the bedroom he threw himself on the bed and curled up. He tried to keep it out. He thought of emptiness, darkness, a place of calm where nothing happened.

It was dark and the room was lit up only by the yellow streetlight when she came to him. She comforted him and said she was sorry. She just talked. Eventually he came back. He accepted her reassurances that it would be all right. She promised not to let him down again. Slowly he accepted that certainty could be restored. All he had to do was to get through tonight, and start over again tomorrow.

Tomorrow he would start the routine again. He would have his usual breakfast, go for a walk in the Waterworks, and then to the community centre. Tomorrow was fish night and he knew he would have that for his supper. It would be OK tomorrow. There would be certainty and he would cope. It was the certainty that kept him sane, and he had to hang on for just four more years.

He could do that.

— *XII* —

Be Brave

HE SOMETIMES WISHED that he had taken a dog when one was offered to him. Like now, when he wanted to cross the road and could not find a pedestrian crossing. He was at the kerb. He knew that, but all he could hear was the dull roar of traffic with no letup. He could of course ask for help, but like refusing the dog, he was too proud and wanted his independence, even if, like now, that was an illusion. He could hear people walking past him and expected someone to stop and offer assistance. That would be all right: that would not be an affront to his dignity. Couldn't these bloody people see his white cane? Yes, a dog would be useful on an occasion like this.

He had been blind now for two years but he still could not accept it. It had happened in Belfast when he was serving there. He came from an old army family and becoming a soldier was the natural thing to do, but all the family lore and his training had not prepared him for the reality of Belfast. He did not like to think about his time there. He had been in Northern Ireland for only a few months, his tour of duty cut short by his injury. He was not one of those who talked about his experiences, and on the few occasions that he went to regimental reunions, he felt that his short time in Belfast and this stupid bloody injury did not stack up against the experiences that many of his fellow officers had. The strange thing was, though, that he still thought about Mrs Conway.

It was one of those rare hot sunny days that Belfast did not have enough of. He was a green lieutenant in charge of a patrol being sent out to harass a known Republican. Officially he was gathering community intelligence and the fiction was that he would call into all the flats on that particular floor to ascertain who lived there, what their occupations were, attitude to the security forces, and so on. He had authority to conduct a search if he, or one of his men, thought there was anything suspicious. But the real purpose was to put pressure on Jimmy Conway in the hopes that he might do something stupid. Intelligence sources were certain that he was a big wheel in the IRA in West Belfast. However the brass dressed it up, he was not so naïve as not to realise that this was a raid.

As the two Land Rovers drove down the Falls Road at speed, he reflected that even in the sunshine, Belfast looked a grim place. Terraces of slum houses squatted alongside abandoned factories. Gable walls were marred by painted messages, 'Up the RA', 'Brits out', or occasionally a mural glorifying IRA terrorists. He thought that if he were back home now on a day like this, he would take the MG out, pick up his girlfriend and head off to the coast: a bathe in the sea followed by lunch and a pint in his favourite country pub. Yes, that is what he would be doing if he were back home and not stuck in this dreary, hostile city. His thoughts were interrupted by his sergeant, 'Nearly there, Sir.'

The Divis Flats complex could have been anywhere in any British city. It was a collection of ugly concrete blocks. There was one tower about twenty storeys high where the army had put a look-out post on the roof within days of being deployed in Belfast to keep the peace. The men up there would keep an eye out and warn him if trouble was brewing. An army presence always brought people out and usually ended up in stone throwing or a gun attack. The other blocks were squat buildings containing what were called maisonettes – flats with two floors. They were four storeys high with long balconies on each floor, the so-called streets in the sky beloved of town planners and architects in the 1960s.

It was on the third floor of one of these that Mrs Conway and her two children lived. They had just moved into the Divis Flats about a month before, he learned from the briefing. Raiding her home on a regular basis was routine. It was part of the standard procedure, part of psychological operations. Just like swooping up suspects and holding them in the barracks. They would be given harsh treatment to break

them. Officers like him did not take part in that. It was left to
the NCOs and other ranks to administer beatings and other
physical pressures but an Intellegence Officer would always
be there afterwards to ask the questions. He did not like this
kind of duty because he did not think it was proper warfare,
but he never had the courage to express this opinion to his
messmates.

There was a half chance, a very slim half chance, that
on one of these raids they would catch Conway. Perhaps he
would risk dropping in on his wife for some creature comfort.
Or they might find documentation that he had carelessly
left behind. But the real reason was to make life difficult for
the wife and kids. They were sending a message to Conway
that while he was safely hidden somewhere in the maze of
Victorian terraced streets of West Belfast, the family he'd left
behind were going through hell.

This was the first time that he had been asked to lead a
raid on the Conway household. He'd been briefed in advance
and had seen photographs, but they did not prepare him
for the reality of Mrs Conway. When he barged into the
tiny sitting room, he was struck by her right off. She was a
beautiful woman, and even if she was a good ten years or
more older than him, he could not help but feel attracted.
With her red hair and green eyes, she looked like a picture-
postcard Irish colleen. He had to admit to himself too that
she carried herself well. She did not scream and curse at his
soldiers like plenty of them did, and she did not break down
in self-pitying tears either. She had a self-assurance about her,
a dignity that made him feel diminished. She stood in the
sitting room with a child in each hand, a young boy and girl.
They both looked afraid and kept their eyes on their mother.
She stood straight, defiant. She looked him in the eye and
spoke to him as an equal. She had that Belfast accent but not
like one he'd heard before. She spoke clearly and used words
he didn't think would be in her vocabulary.

He introduced himself, 'Lieutenant Barclay', and briefly
explained why they were here. While the members of his
patrol, supervised by the sergeant, noisily went through the

two-bedroomed flat, he got out his notebook and asked her the routine questions about herself, her husband, his whereabouts, and all that. She replied in a firm voice, not answering the questions but talking to him.

'Look around you,' she said. 'You don't see much, do you? There's not much here in the way of personal belongings, very few photographs, that kind of thing, is there?'

He agreed with her, not sure where she was going with this. The room was so small that he could feel the heat of her body and her breath on his face.

'That's because me, my family, our entire street was burned out by a Loyalist mob last May. Burned out. House after house set on fire while youse Brits looked on. You know when youse came here we were told it was to protect us, to restore peace. It didn't take long before you turned on the Catholics, did it? Within months you started doing the Unionist Party's dirty work for it.'

He listened as she spoke, captivated by her voice and eyes. He was suddenly embarrassed as he felt himself stiffen. He shook off the feeling and continued to ask her about Jimmy Conway. They were interrupted by the sergeant coming into the room. Suddenly she shouted, 'You can't have those. They were my father's!'

He saw that the sergeant was holding a battered pair of binoculars. They were the type that civilian birdwatchers used. The cheap leather case was worn and scratched, the binoculars were scratched too.

'These binoculars belonged to my father. You can't have them,' she said in a calm voice.

'These can be of use to terrorists, Sir,' said the sergeant. 'She's probably a spotter for an IRA sniper, Sir. We should confiscate these field-glasses and arrest the bitch too.'

Barclay knew that the sergeant probably wanted the binoculars as a souvenir, nothing more. He had always let him have his way. Sergeant Briggs was the kind of old soldier that Kipling celebrated. He had seen service in Korea, Cyprus and Aden. Barclay was not long out of Sandhurst and always deferred to him out in the field. The other ranks in their platoon looked to the sergeant for guidance and orders. But this time Barclay felt different. For reasons he couldn't explain to himself, he felt he owed Mrs Conway something. She had suffered this intrusion with dignity, and clearly had suffered in many ways, yet she was calm and beautiful amid it all.

'Put the field-glasses down and assemble the men. We're leaving,' he said.

The sergeant looked at him a moment, sizing him up, and then said slowly and deliberately,

'I think this is material of use to terrorists and we should take this woman in, Sir.'

Barclay realised that by defying Sergeant Briggs he had created a situation. The sergeant had assumed moral leadership of Barclay's platoon and he had let him. Now he wanted to show himself a man in front of Mrs Conway. He knew that he was about to cross a Rubicon and that his relationship with Sergeant Briggs would never be the same.

'No, Sergeant, you will put down those field-glasses and take the men outside. We are leaving now.'

To his surprise, the sergeant meekly set down the binoculars on the shabby little coffee table and called the men. He took out his anger on them, giving them a bollocking as they assembled on the balcony outside the flat.

Barclay turned back to Mrs Conway. She looked him in the eye and said, 'Thank you. I know they're not much and you probably think it's stupid, but they're all I have left to remember my Da by.'

He hesitated, wanting the moment to last longer. It was as if she had him under a spell. He wanted to say something meaningful to her, but a British officer does not apologise to the wife of an IRA man or pass the time of day with her. He vaguely pointed in the direction of the binoculars and said, 'Good day, ma'am.'

It was about a week later that he was leading another patrol, this time on foot, through the same block of flats, he and Sergeant Briggs. In the stairwell one of the squaddies carelessly pulled back the lid of a rubbish chute. All he remembered later was a flash and a loud bang. There was the smell of smoke and burning flesh, the sound of screams.

He awoke in an ambulance, a medical orderly attending to him.

'Don't try to open your eyes, Sir. We've a bandage on them.'

He didn't want to open his eyes. They felt heavy and all he could make out was a kaleidoscopic pattern of red and orange floating about. He felt no pain and couldn't move his limbs. They must have shot him full of morphine.

'My men?' he asked.

The MO hesitated, 'Two dead. Your sergeant and a private. You and two others injured.'

They took him to the Royal Victoria Hospital just up the road from the Divis Flats. He lay in bed feeling weak, his eyes bandaged and a drip in is arm. He wasn't sure of time passing as one day drifted into the next. Then one afternoon, not long after lunch, he heard two Belfast women talking outside his room. No civilians were supposed to be here: it was the military wing. Suddenly, he recognised one voice instantly and called out without thinking, 'Mrs Conway! Is that you?'

'Lieutenant Barclay?' He heard her say.

There was a kerfuffle at the door of his room and an English voice said, 'Sorry, Miss, no civilians allowed.'

'Let her in,' Barclay said, 'I know her.'

Mrs Conway was at his bedside and took hold of his hand. Hers felt soft and warm.

He felt a thrill go through him and wished she would take him in her arms, just hold him.

'Ah Jesus! What happened, son?' she asked with genuine concern.

He briefly told her.

'I'm sorry it had to be you,' she said, 'I appreciate what you did over the binoculars. You don't deserve this.'

'You didn't come here to visit me?' he said as lightly as he could, while deep down he hoped it might be true.

She laughed, 'No, I'm here to see my mammy. She's in and out of this place more often than one of the doctors. Her health's been bad these past few years. She's in for a wee operation. This place is like a maze. I always get lost. I haven't a notion how I ended up in this corridor.'

'Of course,' he replied.

'How are you? How bad is it, son?'

For the first time he realised his true predicament. He would never see again and had no future in the army. His girlfriend would not want him like this, and he had no idea what to do in civilian life. He felt overcome by despair.

'Alice, will you come on. It's getting on and I've to be back to work,' another woman's voice said from the door.

'I have to go,' said Mrs Conway. 'You look after yourself now.'

He said nothing. He was afraid to speak, afraid of all the emotion that might pour out, for he knew that of all the people he had around him since the bomb, only she would understand him.

She took his hand once more and squeezed it, 'Be brave, now, won't you?'

It was funny but that was what he always remembered. Everyone had been very supportive: the staff in the hospital, the medical people in the military, the rehabilitation clinic. His family could not have been better. His chums from the regiment were always there for him. Everyone encouraged him and supported him. He had been through therapy and rehabilitation but somehow all that was not enough. He was literally in a black despair for the first few months after he got back home to England. He had been so bad at times that he was willing to chuck it all in. A simple bullet would do it. He still had his army pistol. But the one thing that kept him going were her words. Whenever he had hovered on the edge of the abyss, he remembered Mrs Conway's face, her green eyes, and heard her say, 'Be brave.'

XIII

Love and Hate

I

I T HAD BEEN A GOOD WEEKEND OVERALL. The weather
had been sunny and warm; they had some nice meals;
enjoyed walks along the seafront; took the ferry out to
Rathlin Island; even the sex had been good. Ballycastle was
where they had spent their honeymoon, and so it seemed
appropriate to come back here for their thirtieth wedding
anniversary. It was hard to believe they had been married that
long. Now it was Monday and they'd be going home. They
had a romantic meal, candlelight and all, the night before. In
the candlelit atmosphere, and the glow of a few glasses of
wine, she thought that overall their marriage was not too bad.
They had no children but they had had good times together;
had got through the ups and downs of life, and survived the
Troubles. Comfortable like an old pair of shoes, she thought.

They didn't have to leave until the evening so they spent
the morning wandering round the shops, stopping for coffee
in the little café they'd come to think of as 'their place'. Barry
suggested that they go for a walk along the beach since the
weather was still good. They walked out to where the beach
ended in a rocky outcrop, and back again, hand in hand. They
were almost back on the paved seafront when Barry asked her
if she minded if he went on ahead. He really had to get to
the loo. There was a public toilet near the pier where they'd
caught the ferry to Rathlin.

'That second cup of coffee in the café is catching up with
me,' he pleaded.

She said OK and off he went.

She watched him bustle off ahead of her along the seafront,
passing other pedestrians and dodging cyclists. Suddenly it

was like she was seeing him for the first time. How ridiculous he looks, she thought. A little man trying to imitate a big man's walk. Strutting like he was a grenadier in his silly shorts and sun-hat too big for him. He was trying to go as fast as he could while maintaining his dignity, but he had to break into a trot as he neared the public toilets.

'Why did I marry him?' she asked herself. She knew why: she thought she loved him. And thirty years ago the Troubles were at their height. There was violence on the streets, neighbours murdered on their doorstep, people burned out of their houses. It felt like the world was collapsing around them, and she was afraid that neither of them would see the week out. They were both eager to consummate their love and if they didn't get married as soon as possible, they may never get the chance. Besides, in marrying him, she became someone. She was no longer Sadie Madigan's wee girl, but Mrs Barry O'Neill.

Suddenly seeing him as he really was made her angry with those thirty years of marriage. He was never handsome but in his youth he had a way about him, and he made her laugh. She couldn't say when she fell out of love with him. Throughout the Troubles, there didn't seem to be the time to think of such things. They hadn't been married too long when her sister and her husband moved in with them in their new house that they'd barely begun to think of as home. They had been burned out of Annalee Street and were given the front room and spare bedroom to live in until they found somewhere else more permanent. What was supposed to be a short-term arrangement went on for months. She didn't resent this, then or now, but it did distract from the business of marriage. The sister and her husband moved out, but there didn't seem to be the time to settle properly into marriage. They were always occupied with something else. For a time, they thought they would be burned out themselves, and they had to cope with bomb scares, army raids, and worse. In the early years of the Troubles, there were nights when they didn't go to bed because of rumours that Loyalists were coming to burn them out. When Barry was at work, she worried about him and she was terrified if a bomb or gun attack was reported on the news. They'd suffered too the trauma of family members being murdered or imprisoned. It just seemed to be one thing after another, until before she knew it decades had passed by, without any thought of where their relationship was going. Things had settled down; there was the IRA ceasefire; and then the Good Friday Agreement. It felt like a great weight had been lifted off them, or a dark cloud removed, she thought. It was like emerging out into the open after years of living in a cave.

She was waiting for him when he came out of the toilet, giving her a sheepish grin. Look at him, she thought, with his little piggy eyes behind his dorky glasses and a nose too big for his face. Why did he bother to wear a short sleeved shirt with those arms? They were like a couple of chicken legs sticking out of his sleeves. How could she ever think he was good looking? How did she ever fall in love with him? He can't even control his bladder.

They stopped at the first bar they came to. There were couples sitting at tables outside on the pavement and they found a free one. They had no sooner sat down than he began to noisily move his chair round.

'What are you doing?' she snapped.

'Trying to get into the shade,' he said.

'You're making a bloody show of yourself, that's what you're doing.'

He said nothing to this but picked up his glass and swallowed a mouthful of beer. After a minute or two of silence, he started up his usual inane chatter. Of course, it's hot; of course that's the bloody sea; and yes I see the little birds, little man!, she felt like saying, yet didn't. But she could see that her silence was getting to him.

She hurried him to drink up and insisted that they go back to the hotel. They didn't have to check out but she felt a need to move. On the way back along the seafront, she kept up the silence and walked as slow as she dared. He had a sore hip – the result of some stupid accident – and preferred to walk in long strides as it was less of a strain on it. She knew he wanted to walk like that now but she was deliberately going slow, delighting in his discomfort. They checked out of the hotel and he put their bags in the car. They would have lunch, and later head back to North Belfast.

Lunch passed off quietly enough but her resentment of him kept growing, and all his attempts at conversation fell flat against her silence. It could not be said that she engineered what happened next but she took the chance when it came. They finished lunch and started off for the hotel car park. She strode ahead, with him behind her, walking stiffly now on his weak hip. She heard him say 'Ciara' but walked on. He said it again but she ignored him. Then he raised his voice, 'Ciara!'

Slowly she stopped and turned to face him. 'Don't you talk to me like that! Shouting at me as if I was a dog! Just say my name. There's no need to shout. I'm not deaf.'

Once she started, she couldn't stop. Years of resentment and frustration poured out as she called him all sorts of names and tore shreds from his self-respect. She noticed a young woman sitting at a nearby bench drinking a can of coke. She had been amused when this little scene started but now her jaw dropped at Ciara's tirade. It was the first time that Ciara had actually seen someone's jaw literally drop. The young woman covered her mouth and looked away. This only encouraged Ciara who had another go at Barry.

He was shocked and hurt as he explained quietly that he had left his jacket at the café. He went back for it and she waited for him by a shop window. He was still too shocked to speak, and she found that she was enjoying his confusion. She gave him the cold shoulder for the rest of the day: she wouldn't speak to him on the way back to the car, or even on the journey home. He had the bemused look of a hurt dog, she thought, and clearly had no idea what to do or say.

When they were well out on the road heading south, he tried to say something, 'I'm sorry. I didn't mean to...'

'Shut up!' she said. 'I'm sick of the way you treat me. What my life could have been if I hadn't been saddled with you.'

She could see he was really upset but didn't care, and lobbed a couple more verbal grenades at him. She tuned the radio to a pop music station and turned it up so as to stop him speaking.

The journey back was much longer than expected, with heavy traffic and roadworks slowing them down, but she didn't mind. She was enjoying her new-found power and his suffering. What an insignificant little man, she thought. He's held me back; given me a dull, ordinary life. Just look at him, moping like a whipped dog. All through the rest of the drive home she kept silent. When they arrived at their front door, he tried to say something but he could barely speak; there was a catch in his voice as if he were about to cry. Once in their house, she dropped her bag on the floor and went off to bed. He meekly followed, saying nothing. When the lights were out, he said good night. She snorted in reply.

'Look love,' he said, 'I don't know what I've done, but if there's anything I can do to make it up, tell me.'

'Don't know what you've done?' she said. 'You've made my life a dull hell. And I'm sick of it. Sick and tired of you.'

She turned her back on him and retreated into the silence of the darkness. She could feel him move to the edge of the bed and lie there, trying to keep still.

Her victory was complete. In the morning, she would tell him to pack his bags and go.

II

H E HAD ENJOYED THE WEEKEND AWAY, despite his early doubts. Ciara had suggested that they take a long weekend in Ballycastle to mark their thirtieth wedding anniversary, but he wasn't sure if he could get the time off work. In the end, it was easy enough to arrange the Monday off. Once he explained that it was their wedding anniversary, there was no problem. Thirty years! Where did the time go? It had been a good weekend overall. The weather had been sunny; they had some good food in a local restaurant; enjoyed walks along the seafront; took the ferry out to Rathlin Island; even the sex had been good. They'd had a nice meal in a

nice restaurant the night before and it sort of reminded him
of being on honeymoon. He felt almost smug in saying to
himself that theirs was a good marriage. Among his friends,
he seemed to be the only one who wasn't always falling out
with his wife, or whose marriage was rocky,

The last day, the Monday, they spent the morning
wandering round the shops, stopping for coffee in the little
café they'd come to think of as 'their place'. They went for a
walk along the beach since it was dry and sunny. They walked
out to where the beach ended in a rocky outcrop, and back
again, hand in hand. They were almost back and on the paved
seafront when he felt a need to go. This had been a problem
recently but he put it down to middle-age. He was determined
that he would hold out until they reached the public toilets
near the pier, but Ciara was walking very slowly, and if he
were to stay with her, he knew he wouldn't make it.

'Do mind, love, if I scoot ahead? I really need to get to
the loo,' he said.

'OK,' she said noncommittally.

He speeded up and headed off. He walked as fast as he
could without running but it wasn't easy. It was like every
other person on the path deliberately got in his way: people
with buggies, people on bikes, people with dogs, toddlers and
the elderly, all blocked his path. He navigated his way through
them but the pressure on his bladder was getting worse. He
got near the pier and sprinted across the carpark into the
toilets. She was waiting for him when he came out. She had
a strange expression on her face but he thought nothing of it.
Sheepishly he apologised for his weak bladder. They walked
up the main street and stopped at the first bar that had a few
tables outside on the pavement. People were sitting at them
enjoying the sun and they sat at a table just being vacated by
a young couple.

He was sideways to the sun and even though he had
sunscreen on, he could feel his right arm burning in the
intense sunlight. He moved his chair round the table into the
shade. The footpath was uneven and the chair scraped loudly
on it.

'What are you doing?' she suddenly snapped.

He was taken aback by her tone and explained that he was just moving his chair.

'You're making a bloody show of yourself. Everyone's looking at you,' she hissed.

People were looking alright, but it was at her. Momentarily, the thought crossed his mind that they were going to have an argument but he dismissed it. As they drank, he kept up the conversation, commenting on what was going on, making the kind of silly remarks that always made her laugh. But she didn't laugh, and his unease grew. When the bill came, it was £6 and he only had a £50 note in his wallet. He knew that she just liked to pay the bill and go, not hang around while the waiter or barman fussed about change, as they always did. He asked her if she had a fiver.

Suddenly she exploded. 'A fiver? You want me to rummage around to see if I've a fiver?'

He explained about the £50 note, but she would not listen. 'You're like an old woman there, fussing over the change! Just give him the fifty. It's his job to change it.'

He did this and apologised to her. She seemed mollified.

On the way back to their hotel – Ciara had wanted to go there right away and check out – she walked beside him in silence. He tried to walk at a comfortable pace. He'd been knocked down by a car when he was eight and damaged his hip. His parents should have taken him to hospital there and then, but people didn't do that in those days. Instead they apologised to the driver for causing him trouble. It got worse as he got older, and by the time he was grown up and went to a doctor about it, it was too late. He found that if he took long strides, it was not so bad, but she was walking very slowly, much slower than she normally did. He slowed down to keep beside her: he didn't want to go dashing off from her twice in the one day. Soon he felt a dull ache in his hip. It was very sore by the time they reached the hotel, and carrying their bags out to the car didn't help. They found a nice café to have lunch and the meal passed off quietly enough. She had another drink but he didn't have one as he was driving. After they had paid the bill, they decided to go back to the hotel and get the car.

She got out of her chair and strode off. Stiffly he got up and tried to catch up with her. He now had a sharp pain in his hip. He'd almost caught her when he realised that he had no jacket with him. Worse, he couldn't remember if he had it with him when they had lunch or if had he left it in the car. He called out to her but she walked on. He called again but she refused to stop. He noticed a young woman sitting on a nearby bench drinking a can of coke. She was watching them and smirked at this scene. Still Ciara strode on. He raised his voice, 'Ciara!'

She turned slowly and looked at him with fury in her eyes. 'Don't you talk to me like that! Shouting at me as if I was a dog! Just say my name. There's no need to shout. I'm not deaf.'

He was stunned. This was the last thing he expected. He saw that the young woman on the bench was shocked and she looked away in embarrassment. He burned with humiliation as he explained to Ciara about his jacket. Meekly he went off to get it and then came back looking for her.

She stood staring in at a shop window waiting for him. In silence she turned and walked up the street. He walked beside her, still burning with humiliation, his stomach a knot of anxiety. He was too scared to speak for fear of unleashing another verbal volley. The rest of the afternoon she gave him the cold shoulder. She wouldn't speak to him on the way back to the car, or even on the journey home.

When they were well out on the road heading south, he tried to say something, 'I'm sorry. I didn't mean to …'

'Shut up!' she said. 'I'm sick of the way you treat me. What my life could have been if I hadn't been saddled with you.'

She could see he was really upset but didn't care, and lobbed a couple more verbal grenades at him. He just couldn't understand what she meant. They had a good marriage, a good life, he thought. And he treated her like a queen. She tuned the radio to a pop music station and turned it up loud.

Hostility radiated off her. He was one knot of anxiety as he tried to figure what had gone wrong. His mind raced and he could only see one outcome: the end of their marriage. Deep down part of him expected this. He had never had much success with women before Ciara and he couldn't believe his luck when she agreed to marry him. His friends joked about not knowing what she saw in him, but he couldn't see it either. Somewhere inside him, he always thought that once she saw the real him, it would be over.

The journey seemed to go on forever. This Monday was a holiday for them, but was a work day for everyone else. There was a lot of traffic on the road and he got stuck behind some slow-moving lorries. There were roadworks on the dual carriageway, and what should have been a two-hour journey turned into a five-hour trek. It was late by the time they reached Belfast, and it was like they hit every red light on the way back to their street. He just wanted to get into their house. He was sure that Ciara would calm down once they were inside. He thought it was possible that there would be an argument. They'd hardly ever argued, and when they did, it usually blew over in no time. But they could not talk like this, as the car crawled from one red light to another. He was feeling sick by the time they got to their front door. He tried again to say something but couldn't get the words out.

When they got inside the house, Ciara dropped her suitcase in the hall and announced she was going to bed. He followed her meekly upstairs. The silent treatment continued. Slowly he got into bed, and when the lights were out he made one more attempt at reconciliation.

'Look, love,' he said, 'I don't know what I've done, but if there's anything I can do to make it up, tell me.'

'Don't know what you've done?' she spat out. 'It's everything. Marriage to you has suffocated me. I could have had a much better life without you. I just don't know why I didn't realise this years ago.'

He was shocked and felt like someone had hit him with a hammer. His stomach churned; his head spun. Such viciousness, such hostility. She had gone out of her way to hurt him as much as if she had stabbed him with a knife. Numbed, he slid across the bed as far as he could go. At the edge of the mattress, he lay there as still as he could for fear of provoking her. He could see no way out.

Tomorrow he would pack his bags and go.

XIV

The Funeral

INN STOPPED IN THE HALL to do the check that he always did before going out: wallet, keys and ID. He knew it was important to always have some form of identification ready in case he was stopped by the Army or RUC. If you couldn't prove who you were or give a good reason for where you were going, they would use that as an excuse to hold you up and give you a grilling. Or worse, drag you off to the barracks for close interrogation. He didn't even want to think about that. So he put his driving licence in his inside jacket pocket, from where he could easily retrieve it, and dropped his car keys into his trouser pocket. He looked at himself in the hall mirror in his suit and black tie. He was on his way to a funeral.

Terry had been to primary school with Finn. One of forty-two boys in the class. They probably would not have been friends except that Terry's family lived three doors down from Finn's. That meant they kept in touch, even after Finn got the Eleven Plus and went to St Malachy's College, while Terry failed and was sent to St Gabriel's, the nearest Catholic secondary school, along with most of the other boys in the district. Terry was a tall, strong, broad-shouldered and good-natured lad. Even after he started grammar school and spent most of his time with his head buried in books, Finn sometimes played out on the street with Terry and some other neighbourhood kids. Unlike Finn, who had only one younger brother and sister, Terry's was a big family, nine in all. As the eldest of the brood, he was a natural leader and assumed that role when they played their street games. Still, he often deferred to Finn because he went to grammar school and so must be smart. Finn didn't mind going along with this.

They saw less of each other after Finn started university. In

his second year, he had moved into a flat on Botanic Avenue
and had lived in the university area ever since. He might run
into Terry now and again when he went across town to have
dinner with his mother or for a holiday like Christmas. While
Finn was concentrating on his studies and was enjoying the
social life in the bars around Queen's University, Terry grew
up, got a job and married. He left behind a widow and two
children when a Loyalist gang gunned him down on his
doorstep.

Even if they didn't see much of each other in later years,
Finn always thought of Terry as a friend. Deep down he
envied him his wife and family. Finn had never settled down
with anyone. And he respected Terry too. He took no interest
in politics and did his best to shield his family from the worst
of the Troubles. He chief concern was his family – not just
his wife and kids, but his aging parents and his brothers and
sisters. He was strong in a lot of ways.

As he drove down University Road to make his way to
North Belfast, Finn remembered one time when he was
grateful for Terry's presence. It was a few years ago now, one
of those hot summers in Belfast when there were constant
riots on the streets and the death toll mounted. Finn was back
staying with his mother until the new university term started.
One evening his whole family was sitting around watching
TV when there was a hammering on the front door and
someone was shouting, 'Everybody out on the street! We're
being attacked!' After a moment's hesitation Finn ran out
onto the street, stopping only long enough to tell his brother,
Brendan, to stay at home and guard the house.

Out in the street, Finn saw that many of the men had
makeshift weapons, a pickaxe handle or a poker. He thought
about going back to get something but, weaponless, he ran
on, caught up in the fevered atmosphere. It was beginning to
get dark but the street lights had not come on yet. Terry was
already there, directing people down towards Manor Street.
Finn could see a melée there already. Local men were fighting
off a gang of intruders. Most of these men wore khaki or
camouflage jackets. They all had their faces covered, some

with white handkerchiefs and others with scarves, a Linfield supporter's scarf seemed to be the most popular. Women stood at their gates, some with children beside them, watching what was going on. A man was shouting, 'They've come to burn us out! They've got petrol bombs!'

As Finn got closer, Terry came up to him. 'They're from the River Streets,' he said. Together they ran to the end of the street and joined in the fight. Finn had always done his best to avoid physical violence and Terry, despite his appearance, was no hard man. For his part, Finn just helped in pulling an attacker off someone or pushing one of them away. He couldn't see what Terry was up to.

Someone must have phoned the RUC, for a few minutes later two grey armoured Land Rovers came from the direction of the Cliftonville Road. The Loyalist mob dispersed as the jeeps approached, running back up to the Loyalist enclave known locally as the River Streets. The RUC men jumped from the Land Rovers and soon lined up along the bottom of the street preventing any pursuit. The streetlights had come on by now and their submachine guns glistened in the off-yellow light. There were angry questions from the residents. What were the RUC doing? Why didn't they arrest the Loyalists? A tall, burly sergeant flanked by two constables stepped forward.

'Can someone tell me what exactly is going on here?' he asked of no one in particular.

The men all began to speak at once until an older man, whom Finn recognised as Mr Murphy, an old neighbour, shouted for silence. Abruptly he grabbed Finn by the shoulder and pushed him forward.

'You speak, son. You're a university boy.'

Reluctantly Finn stepped forward.

'Well, what have you got to say, young man?' the sergeant asked.

Briefly Finn explained what happened. The sergeant looked sceptical.

'They wouldn't just attack for no reason. You must have done something to provoke them.'

His attitude was making Finn angry.

'We were at home minding our own business. I only came out because someone called me.'

'Still. We've nothing to go on,' said the sergeant.

'We know who they are. We can identify them in court if you want,' a man said, coming to stand beside Finn. Other men joined in saying that they knew who had led the attack and could identify others. The sergeant gave a snort and the two constables with him laughed.

'You're Catholics – that's not evidence!' he said. 'Away home now! Or I'll arrest the lot of you.'

'We've done nothing wrong. It was our street that was attacked,' replied Finn.

The sergeant took a step forward.

'Right. I'm taking you in.'

He reached out to grab Finn. There were angry shouts from the crowd.

'No. You can't do that! He's done nothing wrong.' This was Terry who stood towering over Finn, eye to eye with the RUC sergeant. There was an awkward silence for a moment or two. The sergeant stared angrily at Terry, his hand on the revolver at this side. Terry met his stare.

'All right, lads. Back in the vehicles,' the sergeant said.

Finn always felt he owed Terry for that. Who knows how that situation would have worked out without him there?

He was brought back to the present by the sight of an army checkpoint ahead. He slowed down, halting behind the car in front. His respectable appearance and explanation that he was going to a funeral were enough for him to get through with no trouble. He arrived on the Oldpark Road to find that a big crowd was already gathering. Cars were parked on the road above and below the Sacred Heart Church, and he had to park down near the junction of Rosapenna Street. As he got out of his car, he looked across the road at the bookies there. He remembered another funeral he had to attend when a UFF gang had opened fire on it, killing three people. Almost every street corner had some association with death in the Troubles. Two of Finn's uncles were among the victims.

He went inside the church just as Mass was starting, managing to find a space in a pew near the back. He glanced around, recognising neighbours and family. He couldn't see his mother but supposed that she was up near the front. It had been years since he was here, but the building and the prayers were still familiar to him. Finn had given up on the Catholic Church when he was sixteen. It had been the end of a long process of doubt and questioning followed by scepticism and rejection. Over the years of the Troubles, the attitude of the Church only alienated him more. Some priests were all right, but too often the bishops issued statements asking people to support law and order as if the security forces were neutral or, worse, seeming to blame the Catholic community for what was happening to them. Despite this, Finn was still a 'Catholic' which was really just shorthand for whole lot of beliefs and loyalties, and mainly meant that he wasn't a Unionist.

As he looked around the church, he felt like a Catholic alright. He knew he was among his own people. As the congregation intoned the prayers and knelt or stood up in unison, Finn felt a real sense of community. The Loyalists thought that by killing Catholics they would divide the community against itself, make them turn against the IRA. But their murders had the opposite effect. It only reinforced that sense of community, and as it became obvious that so many of these Loyalist killings could only be carried out with the co-operation of the RUC or British Army, few Catholics had any trust in them.

Outside the church, as there was the hiatus while lifts of the coffin were arranged, Finn found himself standing beside Conor Scott's sister Bernie and their mother. Conor had gone to St Malachy's with Finn but had crossed the water to go to a university in London.

'It was good of you to come,' said Bernie.

'Well, I had to pay my respects. It's important to be here at times like this.'

'Yeah, but you came all the way across town to be here.'

She spoke as though South Belfast were a long way away, which in a sense, Finn supposed, it was. The university area was a sort of neutral zone where you didn't have to worry about religious identity and you could walk the streets at night without fear of attack. A far cry from the area he grew up in.

'Terry was my friend. We sort of grew up together.'

'It's very good of you all the same,' said Mrs Scott. 'Conor sent a sympathy card.'

'How's he doing? I haven't heard from him in ages.'

'He's doing fine as far as we know. He doesn't keep in touch,' she said with a hint of bitterness.

Finn took the chance to lose himself in the crowd. He was in no mood for talking. He hated funerals. He had been to the funerals of too many whose life was cut short by a bullet or bomb. He had fought the feeling all morning, had filled his head with thoughts and memories, but the sight of Terry's coffin being carried by his brothers, with his shattered widow and children walking behind, triggered off the emotions he had been trying to suppress. He remembered when his Uncle Christy had been murdered. It was in the early years of the Troubles. A UVF gang drove into his street one night. Uncle Christy's was the only one whose front door wasn't closed. Aunt Liz was out with friends and he was at home babysitting. He left the front door open and the lights on for her. The men who killed him fired blindly through the frosted glass of the inner door when Christy came out to answer it. Only one bullet hit him, but one was enough. He died hours later in hospital after doctors had removed the bullet from his brain and tried to save his life.

Finn still had nightmares about taking the phone call to hear that Uncle Christy was shot, and seeing his mother collapse onto a sofa in shock when he told her. Then hours later word came through that Christy had died. Finn saw again as men, hard men, Uncle Christy's brothers-in-law and friends, cried at his funeral, heard again the wails of Aunt Liz and his own aunts as the coffin was taken from the house, and the silent grief of his granny unable to take it all in.

Seeing Terry's wife sobbing into a handkerchief, while her two children walked beside her in bewildered silence, and Terry's parents and his brothers and sisters walking alongside her, some expressing their grief in silence, others crying, brought it all back.

Finn followed the coffin until it was put into the back of the hearse. The cortege proceeded slowly down the Oldpark Road and he stopped when he got to his car. He was not surprised to see his mother standing beside it.

'I thought you'd be here,' she said. 'Are you coming home for lunch?'

He said yes and let her into the car.

'There's a lot more cars in this street than there used to be when I was growing up,' he said as they pulled up outside his old front door. 'I'm lucky to get parking so close.'

'There's plenty of changes since you went to live on the other side of town. There's hardly any of the old neighbours left. The Housing Executive is buying up the houses and moving people in from all over Belfast. And some of them are not very respectable.'

'Did they not make you an offer?'

'Sure, they did, but I turned them down. I know this house is a bit big for me since your father died and you all moved out, but it's been my home for near on thirty years, ever since we got married. I'll see my days out here.'

His mother talked like an old woman but she was only in her early fifties. Life has worn her down, Finn thought. All those years when she had to work at the stitching, supporting him and his brother and sister after his dad had died. That was as well as doing all the washing and cooking, and spending most Saturdays looking after her own mother. And the Troubles too. Finn wasn't the only one with bad nights. His mother had lived through those deaths too and endured violence on her own doorstep and harassment by the security forces. Finn always felt guilty at moving to the university area and leaving her to cope on her own with Brendan and Helen, but it had been his mother's idea: 'I don't want you traipsing across town at night with them Shankill Butchers lifting people off the streets.' He had resisted at first but when a couple of his friends moved into university accommodation, he changed his mind. Thank God, the days of the Shankill

Butchers' kidnapping Catholics and torturing them to death had long gone.

He sat at his mother's kitchen table while she fried some fish fingers and chips for him. He was still a wee boy in her eyes and this was one of his favourite meals when he was young.

'That was a big turnout today, wasn't it?' she said.

'Sure was, but that was no surprise. Terry was well liked and people want to show their solidarity for a murder victim.'

'It's awful sad all the same. To think a big handsome man like him shot like a dog in the street. And him leaving behind that poor wee girl and two wee'ans.'

'I know. It's shocking,' he said, 'but he's not the first, and I don't suppose he'll be the last before all this is over.'

'It's a pity you weren't here for the wake. There was a big turnout for that too. I brought Mrs Morgan down some sandwiches and somebody had made a big pot of stew. Sad to say there was too much drink taken by some of the fellas, but, sure, what can you say at a time like that?'

His mother was a lifelong Pioneer of Total Abstinence. She had taken the pledge when she was twelve and had never touched a drop of alcohol in her life.

'The family's taking it awful bad. You should have seen the grown men crying. At least it's a comfort to them knowing that a priest performed the last rites for Terry when he got to the hospital. At least he died in the arms of the Church.'

Finn said nothing to this. He had no idea if Terry was still a practising Catholic but he knew it would mean something to his parents, who were devout.

'It's great too to see the support they got from their neighbours. They haven't had to lift a finger the past few days. I know you'll laugh at this but I find it a comfort too. It's like when those Loyalists kill one of us, it's a crime committed against us all.'

'I'm not laughing,' he said.

'You know with the army in this street every day, and these murders, it's like North Belfast is under siege. You're lucky to be living where you are. I'm glad I told you to go. God knows, you might be dead by now as well.'

'I know, Mammy. I know I'm lucky.'

'Do you want something sweet? I baked an apple cake yesterday,' she asked as she took his plate away.

'Just a small slice. And then I have to go.'

'Back to work is it?'

'Yes.'

'Well, it was good to see you. It's great that you have that job. I'm always bumming about you.'

'Mammy, you'll be making me blush.'

'Sure, what harm?'

'I really have to go.'

He drove back to his flat in University Street which he could never really think of as home. As he crossed that invisible, indefinable line between North Belfast and the city centre, he felt relief at leaving all that sorrow and suffering behind.

XV

A Lost Love

I N RETROSPECT, it would have been wiser not to tell her what he was thinking at that moment. Even the happiest of wives is apt to be jealous of an old girlfriend, even one designated to the past as a 'lost love', especially a wife who claims not to have a lost love in her past. They were having Sunday lunch in their local pub. He wasn't paying much attention to the soundtrack coming out of the speakers until Stephen Tin Tin Duffy's 'Icing On The Cake' came on. Instantly he was transported back to that wet summer of 1985, and Julia. Like a drowning man, the events of that summer, from first meeting to last goodbye, flashed before his eyes.

'What are you thinking about?' she asked.

'Oh just remembering,' he said.

'Remembering what? I've never seen that look on your face before.'

'A look?'

'Yes. All dreamy but somehow sad.'

'It's a girl I used to know. That was our song.'

'You had a song? It must have been serious.'

'Yes, it was. She was my first true love. My lost love.'

The atmosphere turned frosty after this revelation, not helped by his reluctance to say more. There are some memories and emotions that you can't explain to your wife, even if she is the one woman you love.

He met Julia in May of 1985. He might never have met her at all. A friend had invited him to come along to birthday drinks for another friend in The Regency. He had graduated with his Masters from Queen's University a few months before, and had still to find a job. He thought that with his degrees a job would be easy to find, but that was not the case. He could have gone back to Queen's to do a teaching diploma except he was determined not to be a teacher. He didn't mind living on the dole, so long as it was temporary, but it did not leave him with much money and his social life was severely curtailed. He felt dispirited at his situation and thought that a few drinks with friends would cheer him up. He checked his wallet and reckoned he had just about enough money to pass himself if they were only going to the pub for a few drinks.

He had eaten his dinner and, looking out at the rain, decided he would not bother going out; after all it was only the birthday of the friend of a friend. He sat down to watch television and was flicking through the channels when suddenly he changed his mind. Putting on his parka and pulling the hood up against the rain, he set off for The Regency bar, which was only a short walk away. There were about a dozen people there already, sitting at a couple of tables at the back of the room. Most of them he knew. He did not even notice Julia at first. His attention was taken up by a beautiful blonde, who was the centre of attention for all the men there. He couldn't figure out whose birthday it was, but was enjoying the occasion anyway. As the crowd shuffled around, people moving from one seat to another to talk to someone else, he found himself sitting next to this woman he had not seen before.

She was slightly built with glossy brown hair cut in pageboy style, but it was her green eyes he noticed first. He thought of emeralds and was enchanted by her.

'We haven't been introduced. I'm Finn Conlyn.'

'Julia Pollock,' she said taking his hand. 'What sort of name is Finn?'

He laughed, 'With a name like Pollock, you're in no position to laugh at Finn. It's short for Finbar.'

'Is that Gaelic?' she asked. 'What does it mean?'

'The Fair-haired one,' he explained.

'How exotic! But you're not blond. More light brown.'

'My parents honeymooned in Cork,' he explained. 'There's a St Finbar's cathedral there. My mam liked the name.'

And so it went on. It was like there was no one else in the room, as he and Julia talked about their favourite books, films, music, and the rest. They were caught unawares when the lights in the bar began to flash on and off to signal it was closing time.

Outside in the street, there was a suggestion of getting a takeaway and carrying on the party in someone's flat.

'I'm going to go on home,' Julia said. 'My Dad doesn't like me to be out late.'

'Can I walk you to the taxi rank?' Finn asked. She said OK.

This did not take long as the taxi office was just behind The Regency, but Julia had to wait for a taxi, so Finn sat with her and they carried on talking until her name was called. Outside, even though the rain was falling heavily, she stood beside the taxi and said, 'Good night, fair-haired one.' and kissed him full on the lips, which he eagerly returned. Then she got into the taxi. As it drove off, Finn shouted, 'Can I see you again? How can I contact you?'

But it was too late. Her taxi was disappearing out of sight and he felt like an eejit for not asking her earlier. Despite this, he had hopes that he would see her again. He was lighthearted as he skipped home through the rain, sure for no good reason that he had met the one.

The next day, Finn sought out Adam, the friend who had invited him to The Regency, but Adam had no idea who Julia was or where she lived. 'She was just the friend of a friend, I suppose,' he said.

Finn didn't know who else to ask about Julia but his conviction that he would see her again meant he wasn't dispirited. His faith was vindicated when a postcard came through his letterbox the following Wednesday. On the front was a photograph of the Eiffel Tower but it had been posted in Belfast. The message read:

'Hi Finn, got your address off Gerry. I'll be in the Bot next Saturday at 2 o'clock if you're interested. X'

It could only be from Julia, although he wasn't sure who Gerry was.

Finn felt elated and excited at the thought of seeing Julia again. The truth was that he had not much experience with girls. He'd been a bookish teenager who had withdrawn into himself when his father died. He'd always been unsure around girls, and going to an all-boys school did not help. He only really got to know girls when he went to Queen's. There were girls in his class and his friends had girlfriends. He did date a few but there was nothing serious in any of these relationships. Then the shock of his Uncle Christy being murdered at the end of his first year knocked him back again. He became withdrawn once more and drank more than he should have. All this was compounded when Uncle Jimmy was murdered the following year. For a long time, he was reclusive and alcoholic. In the four years since, the psychological damage had healed to some extent and he was able to relax and have a good time. He still didn't have much success with women though, but that did not stop him dreaming of meeting 'the right one'.

That Saturday, he arrived in the Bot, the popular name for The Botanic Inn on the Malone Road, at exactly fifteen minutes after two. He had agonised over this during the week. If he was early and arrived before Julia, he might appear too keen, and a little desperate. If he arrived exactly on time, that might appear a bit compulsive. He decided that arriving fifteen minutes later would be about right. He reckoned that he would not appear desperate or obsessed about being punctual, but would be early enough so that Julia would not give up waiting on him.

'Gosh, there you are!' she said when he approached the table where she was sitting. 'I was afraid I'd missed you. I only just got here myself.'

She stood up and he pecked her proffered cheek. He felt a thrill run through him just like the first time they'd met and he wasn't sure how to act. However, any awkwardness was soon gone. Julia did most of the talking, and Finn listened. Time flew and, before he knew it, she was suggesting that they go for something to eat together. Luckily Finn had got his latest unemployment cheque a few days earlier.

And that was the beginning of their romance. They saw each other as much as they could after that. Julia was a newly qualified social worker, so she was only free at weekends. She lived with her parents and her dad was strict so there were very few late nights. They made love for the first time on a Sunday afternoon after they had gone for a walk in the Botanic Gardens. A heavy rain shower came out of nowhere and they ran back to Finn's place on Ireton Street. They began kissing on the stairs leading up to his flat, and going to bed together just seemed natural.

It continued like this over the following weeks. They slipped into a comfortable routine without realising it. They met on Saturday afternoon and had lunch together before going to the cinema, window-shopping in town, or strolling through the Botanic Gardens. They made love while it was still light and usually Julia went home with the promise to meet the next day. After she had got to know him better and to trust him, she arranged an alibi with one of her friends so that she could stay the night with Finn once in a while.

One rainy Sunday afternoon when it was too wet to go out, they were sitting together on the sofa when Finn said, 'I don't know much about you really. Like, what are your parents like? Do you have any brothers or sisters?'

'I've two brothers – I'm the youngest. My parents are just ordinary people. Except they're very devout. Mum and Dad take their religion seriously. Dad reads part of the Bible every night before going to bed. They go to church every Sunday and won't watch television until after our Sunday dinner. When we were kids, Dad would read us the Bible every Sunday afternoon.'

'Jesus, it didn't do you much good did it? Ye huzzy.'

'Don't blaspheme,' Julia said.

'Sorry.'

'I'm not joking. We were serious about religion when we were growing up. We weren't allowed to mix with heretics like you,' she laughed. 'In fact, you're the first Catholic I've really got to know well... And what about you? What's your family like?'

'I'm the oldest. I've a younger brother and sister. My dad died when I was twelve, so my mammy's been on her own since then. She'd get on with your folks. She's very religious, says the rosary, and is a member of the Legion of Mary. Of course, your dad probably doesn't approve of idol worship.'

'What's the Legion of Mary? It sounds military.'

'Well they are militant. Mary the Mother of God. They pray and do good deeds. You know. They feed the poor, visit the sick, that sort of thing. Mam helps out in a hostel for fallen women on the Cliftonville Road.'

'Fallen women?' Julia laughed.

'Well, that's what my mammy calls them. She's quite innocent in a way.'

Another time, when they had been to the cinema and were walking home, an RUC patrol of two armoured jeeps came towards them. The Land Rovers slowed down as they neared the young couple holding hands. Finn went tense and involuntarily gripped Julia's hand tighter. He breathed a sigh of relief when they drove on.

'Something wrong?' asked Julia.

'The RUC,' said Finn. 'They always make me nervous.'

'My dad's a policeman,' she said. 'He's a sergeant in the RUC.'

'An RUC man?' said Finn, shocked.

'Yeah, he's been in the force for years. My older brother's a police constable too, and my other brother is in the army.'

'Does your family know that you're sleeping with the enemy? I'm from North Belfast, don't forget. Where I come from, the RUC is not exactly welcome. They're not the police to us.'

'Don't joke,' she said. 'My dad hates Catholics. He'd kill you if he ever found out.'

'Now you tell me,' Finn said, only half joking.

'My dad's best friend was killed by the IRA and Dad almost died. They were in a patrol car together when an IRA landmine went off under it. It blew the car off the road and it landed upside down. His friend, Johnny, was killed instantly. Dad's still got the scars from where they pulled out the shrapnel.'

'I'm sorry to hear that,' said Finn, 'but there is a war going on. We all know people who've been killed. I don't hate all Prods because my uncles were murdered.'

'Oh, you never told me that,' concern in her voice.

'I don't like to talk about it,' he said.

'God, this place!' Julia said. 'Why are things so complicated?'

'This does change things, doesn't it?' he said.

'There's only one thing for it then,' she paused, 'we'll just have to make sure that they never find out!'

'Jesus, I thought you were going to say goodbye.'

'No, not yet. I'll give you another week or two, and then we'll see,' she joked.

They stayed together for more than a week or two. Finn had never known happiness like this. It was more than that; it was contentment. His time with Julia was the best in his life. He lost track of the weeks passing and was surprised to discover that it was July already. July meant the Twelfth, that annual orgy of Orange bigotry. There'd always been disturbances around the Twelfth when members of the Orange Order set bonfires alight and marched provocatively close to Catholic areas, or through them if they could. Finn and his family usually went to the Republic for the Twelfth fortnight rather than live through that nightmare, but this year he'd opted out of the family holiday. When Julia said she wouldn't be able to see him for a few days, he knew it was because of the Twelfth and accepted it without question. He probably didn't want to know what she'd be involved in. So they arranged to meet again once things had quitened down.

Finn borrowed his brother's car. It was Volkswagen Beetle, his pride and joy, but Finn had asked Brendan nicely and explained there was a girl involved. He and Julia had decided to spend the day on the Antrim coast, a special day out as they hadn't seen each other for a while because of the Twelfth. The sun shone as they drove up the coast road to Portrush. They had fun riding the dodgems and the roller coaster; they got ice-cream and candy floss; they walked arm in arm along the seafront. They drove home happy and tired after a great day out. Finn chose the main road for coming home. It would be quicker and give them the chance to go out for something to eat. Julia had arranged to stay the night with him, a perfect end to a perfect day, he thought. The journey went well until they came upon an RUC checkpoint a few miles north of Belfast. There were not too many cars ahead of them and soon they were alongside the armoured grey Land Rovers and heavily armed RUC men.

A tall RUC man was examining the cars. Finn rolled down his window and smiled politely as he stopped alongside him. The RUC man leaned into the window.

'Driving licence, sir,' he said.

Finn handed over his licence. Without looking at it, the RUC man suddenly said, 'Julia!'

Oh no, thought Finn, her brother!

'What are you doing here?' the RUC man asked.

'Hello, Todd. We're just out for a wee jaunt. It's such a lovely day.'

'Ach aye,' said Todd, 'and is this your young man, then?'

'Oh God, no. He's just a friend, like.'

Todd looked at Finn's driving licence.

'Since you're with the wee lady here, I'll let you go with no bother, Finbar,' he said with a chuckle.

Once they were clear, Finn said, 'The fabled RUC sense of humour.'

'It's no joke, Finn,' said Julia. 'That's my brother's mate. They hang out drinking together.'

'So, what's your problem? I'm just a friend,' said Finn imitating the RUC man's chuckle.

'Don't you see? He'll tell Henry, and Henry'll tell my dad that I'm seeing a Taig. All hell will break loose.'

'Maybe he'll think I'm one of your lot,' said Finn hopefully.

'With a name like Finbar Conlyn? I know Todd's not the brightest but he's not that thick.'

The end came soon after that. They'd met on Sunday for brunch at a place on the Stranmillis Road and took a walk in the Botanic Gardens afterwards. Finn thought that Julia was quieter than usual but did not attach much importance to it. They went back to his flat and made love. As they lay side by side afterwards, Julia began to cry softly.

'I wasn't that bad, was I?' he said.

'Finn,' she said.

'Oh my God. You sound like you've just got bad news, or that you are going to tell me bad news.'

'Oh, Finn,' she whispered.

'For god's sake, Julia, say something,' he pleaded.

She hesitated, sniffed back a tear and said, 'We can't go on like this.'

'Like what? It's been OK so far hasn't it? I was even working up to ask—'

'Don't say that,' she interrupted. 'This has got to be our last time together.'

'What? What do you mean?'

'It's not you. It's not me. It's us,' Julia said.

'What does that mean?'

'You remember Todd? The policeman at the checkpoint a couple of weeks ago.'

'Oh aye, I remember him alright.'

'Well, like I said, he told Henry and Henry told our Dad.'

'And?'

'He blew his top. I've never seen him so angry. He called me all sorts of names. And Henry wasn't much better. Their anger is more than I can take. We can't go on like this.'

'Look, I could meet them. Talk to them. Show them I'm a human being.'

'Dad was angry but Henry said he'd shoot you on sight.'

'Jesus, are you serious?'

'Yes,' she said quietly.

He watched her dress without saying a word. Her silence was too powerful to interrupt. As she left the bedroom, he pulled on a pair of jeans and followed her downstairs. At the hall door, he said, 'Can't we work this out? We could leave... go to England.'

'No, it's not that simple. They're my family. Anyway, Dad would track us down. And there's Eric, too. He's in the army.'

Finn stood in silence staring at the closed door. His world had collapsed around him and he just stood there in his jeans, feeling he did not know what. It was like all the bad things that had happened in his life, all the beatings, all the deaths, were happening all at once. He felt like a wee boy again, vulnerable in a world he couldn't control. The image of her tear-soaked face was in front of him. How could she just walk away?

Years passed and the wound healed over, if the pain was still there underneath. Finn learned to live again and even to love. He had a couple of lovers before Maeve, but only she had filled the void left by Julia. Their marriage was a happy one and Finn was content. And yet all it took was one silly pop song to bring it all back.

XVI

Paschal

FINN DECIDED to walk over to the Falls Road and get a black taxi up to Andersonstown. It was not too far to go down University Road, through the Loyalist district of Sandy Row, and onto the bottom of the Falls where he could get a black taxi up to where the nursing home was. It looked like there might be rain, but he didn't mind getting wet. He had only learned last week through a mutual acquaintance that Paschal was in the nursing home, recuperating after an operation. He felt obliged to go and see him. He was an old friend.

The black taxi was full when he got into it. They were women of all ages, gossiping away to each other. The black taxis on the Falls Road were known as the People's Taxis or the IRA transport corps, depending on who was talking. When the city council withdrew the bus service in West Belfast – after all, they were burning the buses – some locals got together and brought over a load of taxis from London. The taxis ran up and down the road filling the gap left by the absent buses, except they were handier because they stopped where you asked them to. Finn got a few suspicious glances. It was years since he'd been on the Falls, not since his Granny died. An old woman sitting in the opposite corner was looking at him closely,

'Are you one of the Conlyns?' she said.

'Aye. The Masserene Street Conlyns.'

'Ach, I know you now. Are you Christy's son?'

'No. My dad was Pat.'

'Right enough. You're the spit of him. I knew your granny well, so I did. We were great friends. We used to go to the bingo together. I mind your poor Uncle Christy, God rest him.'

At this revelation, the atmosphere in the cab changed and Finn was drawn into the conversation. When it came to his place, he tapped the glass partition behind the driver and gave him 50*p* when he got out.

It was a short walk from there to the nursing home. The receptionist gave a knowing smile when Finn asked for Paschal, and directed him through a nearby door and along a corridor to the conservatory. 'That's where he usually is at this time of day,' she said. Finn followed her directions. He felt slightly awkward coming empty-handed, but what could he bring? Flowers were alright for a woman, or chocolates, but a bottle of whiskey was out of the question here. He'd thought of a book, but Paschal was always too restless to read.

Paschal had come into Finn's life as unexpected as snow in July and as energetic as a whirlwind. Finn had never known anyone with so much nervous energy. Paschal never settled but was always on his feet, pacing up and down as he talked, only stopping talking to pull on his cigarette. That was what gave him the cancer in the end. At the time, Finn had just been appointed editor of *Over The Bridge*, a small arts magazine that a Minister in the Northern Ireland Office thought would make a good vehicle for community relations, helping Protestant and Catholic understand each other. The funding he arranged through the NIO's Community Relations Unit was generous but not adequate. There was enough to pay Finn's modest salary but sales and advertising revenue were supposed to cover the rest of the costs. Finn had persuaded a friend who was out of a job to look after sales but Kate couldn't find time to sell advertisements as well. Finn had put the word out among people he knew in publishing that he was looking for someone, but with no luck so far.

One Friday afternoon, just as Finn was deciding to close up and go home, his office door suddenly burst open. A man dressed in a suit from the 1980s and sporting a moustache of the same vintage strode in. He was tall and thin, probably in his fifties, about twenty years older than Finn but he wasn't sure.

'Are you looking for someone to sell advertising?' he asked in a business-like manner.

'Yes,' said Finn slightly confused.

'I'm glad to hear that. I was in the dole office this morning waiting for an interview when the fella next to me handed me this magazine he'd just finished reading. It was yours – love the name by the way – and as I read through it, I saw that there weren't too many ads in it. Paschal, I said to myself – by the way, my name's Paschal – this outfit could do with someone to sell adverts. So here I am.'

Finn thought this was either the work of fate or some cock and bull story.

All the while, Paschal paced up and down the room, waving his hands, his jacket flapping about him. Finally sitting down, he explained that he had just returned from England where he'd been working in the construction industry for one of the big firms. He'd had enough of that business and fancied a change. The chance to sell advertisements for an arts magazine appealed to him. Finn decided he had nothing to lose and offered Paschal the job. He could only offer a modest retainer and commission on the advertisements he sold, but Paschal seemed happy with that. Finn suspected that he would still go on signing on the dole and receiving unemployment benefit, but didn't want to know. He invited Paschal for a pint to seal the deal, and that was the first of many they shared of an evening after they closed the office. Sometimes Kate, who was mostly out on the road drumming up trade, would join them. Finn always thought it strange that they kept the magazine going with only the three of them. Once, after a pint or two, Paschal said, 'Does something about this setup not strike you as odd, Finn?'

'What do you mean, Paschal?'

'Well, *Over The Bridge* is supposed to be cross-community, bringing Prod and Taig together, right?'

'True, it is.'

'Well how come the only people who work for it, you, me and Kate, are all Catholics?'

'Well, I guess it's because we're the artistic ones!'

'Jesus! Have you seen the state of their murals?' said Kate. They all laughed.

Paschal was full of stories and often spoke of his time in England. He was site manager for one of the big construction companies, and, to hear him tell it, was involved in some of the biggest infrastructure projects in recent years. One time, when was reading the newspaper before settling down to work, Paschal said out of the blue, 'The British and their queen. God save us!'

Finn said nothing but felt a story was coming on.

'Years ago, I was working on the G-Mex Centre in Manchester, and one day near the end of the construction phase, the Queen came for a visit. Oh there was a big fuss over that. We were all given instructions about where to stand and how to behave. And you know what? They even put in a special Portaloo for her. No kidding. It was no ordinary Portloo but was all painted up real fancy and had special fixtures and fittings, just in case Her Majesty needed to take a Jimmy Riddle. The upshot was that Her Majesty didn't need to avail of the facilities, but the people there treated it like it was some kind of shrine. As soon as the Queen was off the site, didn't a digger come along and demolish the thing. Not a scrap of that Portaloo was left. It was like they believed that because it had been set aside for Her Majesty, no mere mortal could use it, even though the royal arse never came in contact with it. And the English people look down on so-called primitive people elsewhere in the world.'

'Did you meet the Queen, then?' Finn asked.

'Ach aye. I was in the line that she came along. Just shaking hands and saying, "How do you do?" I shook her hand alright but I did not bow my head. It was embarrassing. All the women curtsied and the men bowed their heads when presented to her. I got into hot water over that. The chief called me in and admonished me for not showing due respect to Her Majesty. I told him that I was a freeborn Irishman and citizen of a republic, and I don't bow to anyone. Of course, I would bow to the Pope – but I'm not likely to meet him!'

Paschal did make a real difference. He devised schemes to bring in adverts and once he set his sight on a potential customer, never gave up until he had got them to buy an advert, no matter how small. Within six months, there was enough revenue coming in to cover all the magazine's costs and pay Paschal a reasonable fee. Although he was very different from Finn, talkative and daring where Finn was quiet and cautious, they became good friends. They would end most days with a drink in a local bar and sometimes meet for lunch on a Saturday. However, *Over The Bridge* only lasted three years. A new Northern Ireland Minister was all for supporting sport, and Finn had to find another job once the decision was made to close the magazine down. That meant that Paschal was at a loose end again but he was optimistic that he would find something.

'After all, I didn't waste my time with *Over The Bridge*. I made a few useful contacts and I'm pretty sure that one of them could use my services.'

Finn and Paschal drifted apart and they didn't see so much of each other. Whenever their paths crossed, their old familiarity came back in an instant. Paschal was still full of stories and they usually ended up in a pub for a drink or two. Finn was never entirely sure what Paschal was working at, but he seemed to be doing all right. It came as a shock to hear that he was in the nursing home.

Finn stood at the door to the conservatory and looked around. It was a big room, full of potted plants of various sizes, shapes, and colours. Only a few of the chairs and benches were occupied: old men and women reading or nodding off. It took Finn some time to recognise Paschal. He was sitting in a wheelchair at the far end of the room staring out at the garden where the rain was teeming down now. He was in a mousy-coloured dressing gown and had a comfy-looking tartan blanket across his knees. His hair was grey and thinning. His slight frame was even slighter, and his eyes were sunk into his head. Finn approached him cautiously. Paschal turned his head as Finn got close, and gave him a big smile.

'Finn! What kept you? I was expecting you before this,' he said with a twinkle in his eye.

'Good to see you, Paschal. How are you doing?'

'Pull up a chair. Make yourself comfortable. How'd you

know I was here? I asked Paul to see if he could contact you to let you know, but no dice. You were lying low.'

'I came as soon as I heard. An operation was it?'

'Aye, they had to take something out of my lungs,' Paschal tapped his chest. 'You were right. I should've given up smoking.'

'Sure, it was no use talking to you,' Finn said as lightly as he could.

'What are doing with yourself? Still editing?'

Finn filled Paschal in on all that he had been doing since they'd left *Over The Bridge*, and about his new job.

'You know, I've been thinking about how we met,' said Paschal. 'You were mad to take me on, you know.'

'I know but it worked out didn't it?'

'It did. You know being in here gives you time to think. Just before you arrived, I was remembering coming back to Belfast after working across the water. Was I mad or what? Anyone with a titter of wit was leaving, and here was me coming back. Ach, well. I thought it was time I got to know Paul, my son, before he grew up. He'd turned thirteen and was going to become a man without me ever really knowing him. You know I'd no idea what the Falls was like. I grew up there and it was a great place, a bit rough, mind you, but the people were the salt of the earth. I came back to a war zone.

'I remember going out to take a look around just after I got back. There was some kind of protest going on. I can't remember what for, but a gang of young fellas were out on the road hijacking buses and vans, and setting them on fire. Well, sure weren't all these people standing around watching like it was the circus or something? I spotted an old mucker of mine and went up to stand beside him, where we had a good view of the show.

'Next thing the parish priest appears on the scene and starts shouting at the boys to stop. They just ignored him, told him it was none of his business. So he's standing there, shocked like, and looking about him. Then he comes up to me and says, "Will you do something?"

' "Father," I says, "it has nothing to do with me."

' "Ach come on," he says, "in the name of God, call off your boys."

'I was shocked. What'd he mean? My boys? Then Paddy, my mucker, standing next to me laughs fit to burst, "Do you not see?" he says, "He thinks you're the OC!"

'Well do you know what it was? I'd only came home from England and thinking I was looking very smart in my black leather trench coat and sunglasses, never thinking that I looked like an IRA man. That daft priest thought I was an officer in the IRA! Well, if he thought that, some trigger-happy Brit might think the same. I went straight home and put that coat in my wardrobe and it's never seen the light of day since.'

Paddy laughed but it didn't last long as soon he was struggling for breath.

'Should I get a nurse?' Finn asked.

Paschal shook his head as he brought his breathing under control.

'No need,' he gasped. 'I'm OK.'

Finn watched his laboured breathing, not sure if he should do something.

'I could do with a cup of tea,' said Paschal. 'It must be nearly three.'

On cue, an attendant appeared pushing a tea trolley from resident to resident. She knew them all by name and just how they liked their tea.

'Here you are, Paschal. A cup of tea, milk and two sugars?'

'Thanks, love. You're an angel. What are you having, Finn?'

Finn was persuaded to have a cup of black tea and a chocolate biscuit.

'I miss having an aul puff with my tea, all the same,' said Paschal. 'It doesn't taste the same without one. But my cigarette days are over,' he said wistfully, 'and the pints too. I'll never have another Guinness. Doctor's orders.'

'Ach, sure, you'll be the healthier for it.'

'I know. I sometimes wonder if coming back here was the thing to do. I could have taken Paul back to England.

But he wouldn't leave his Ma, even though she showed little interest in him. As soon as I was back, she was happy enough to saddle me with the lad. Said it was my turn after all those years of being away. I didn't mind – he was a teenager by then and could more or less look after himself. But he wanted to stay close to his Ma, so going across the water was out of the question.'

'Well, it all worked out OK, didn't it?'

'Still we've had some scrapes over the years. What with the Troubles, like. Did I ever tell you about that time we were trapped in Kelly's Cellars?'

Finn had heard this story before many times. It was one of Paschal's favourites.

'No. What happened?' he said.

'Well I took the young fella, Paul, into town to get a new pair of shoes. That was simple enough and then we decided to call into Kelly's Cellars off Royal Avenue for a pint before heading back up the Falls. It was very quiet for a Saturday. That place was usually buzzing, and I know it always had a bit of a reputation but it was one of my favourite places to have a drink. We sat at the bar enjoying our pints. That was fine until these two young guys came in. They looked a bit rough, I have to say, and it turns out they were from North Belfast – you know what you North Belfast ones is like. Eh? With the whole bar to choose from, they came and stood not two feet away from us. Well, you should have heard them talk. Effing and blinding. Their sole topic of conversation seemed to be fights they were in. The damage they did to this fella; how they sent this one to hospital; the bars they wrecked; and so on. Well I looked at Paul and he looked at me, and we got up and went to a table at the far end of the room.

'Then we hear this music outside and chanting and cheering. The barman explained that there was an Orange march on that afternoon. Fuck, if we'd known that we'd have stayed at home. No wonder Kelly's Cellars was near empty. There was nothing for it but to sit it out until the Orangemen had gone. So we had another pint. I was just coming back from the bar, a pint in each hand, when there's this commotion outside. I could hear people shouting things like "There's Kelly's Cellars," and "Get them Fenian bastards!" I was worried I can tell you, but before I could set the pints on the table, wasn't the door kicked in and a gang of Orangemen charged into the bar shouting and screaming. Now, in fairness, they weren't dressed in suits and bowler hats, but some of them had blackthorn sticks in their hands. They'd do some damage if one of them hit you. Paul half ducked under the table and I stood there, stunned.

'But then the two boys at the bar – the North Belfast ones – throws their glasses at the Orangemen and charged into them. The whole time they were yelling, "North Belfast! North Belfast! Youse'll never beat North Belfast!" Well you should have seen it, Finn. They were like a couple of berserkers. Even though they were outnumbered three to one in the doorway and with another bunch of Loyalists trying to get in from the street, they got stuck in. Their fists and feet were flying everywhere. They held them Orangemen at the door and even though they were bleeding and bruised, it was like they could feel no pain. "North Belfast!" I don't know how long it lasted. It seemed to go on forever. Then suddenly it all stopped. The Orangemen turned and ran. The two lads just stood there panting, big grins on their faces. One of them manages to say, "North fucking Belfast."

'Next thing didn't the peelers arrive, some big inspector leading them. All of them in riot gear with helmets and truncheons, except this inspector. Didn't the cops grab the lads and say they were under arrest. I got out of my seat and went over to the inspector.

' "Excuse me, inspector," I says, "you shouldn't be arresting those lads. If it hadn't been for them, we could all be dead." I explained in short what had happened, how the Orangemen had invaded the pub, but yer man wasn't interested.

' "We're here to keep the peace," he says, "and we've had a complaint of disorder in this establishment."

'All the while the two North Belfast ones didn't say a word. While the inspector was talking, about half a dozen RUC men cuffed them and dragged them outside.

'I pipes up, "What's your name and number, inspector? I intend to take this up with a higher authority." I had my best posh voice on. But he just looks me up and down, and then, real threatening like, says, "Sit down or I'll take you in as well, Sir." I could see he wasn't joking. So what could I do? I sat down and drank me pint all in one go.'

Paschal fell into another fit of gasping and coughing, but before Finn could do anything, he recovered his composure. Just then, an attendant in bright pink overalls came over, 'Hi Paschal, your tea's nearly ready. I'm afraid you have to go, love. Visiting time is over.'

Finn got to his feet and looked down at Paschal.

'When you get out of here, I'll take you into Kelly's Cellars for a pint – for old time's sake.'

Paschal looked up at him, a look of pity in his eyes,

'Did they not tell you, Finn? When I leave here, it'll be feet first. The operation didn't take. The doc says I've a couple of months at most.'

*   *   *

The funeral took place on another unseasonably bad day, with a leaden sky and the rain pelting down. It reminded Finn of the first time he'd gone to see Paschal in the nursing home. There was a good turn-out in church for the funeral Mass, but then there always is, and Paschal was well liked by his neighbours. There were not so many at the graveside, not surprising as the rain was still coming down in bucketfuls. Finn shook Paul's hand and expressed his condolences. Paul introduced him to his mother, Paschal's ex-wife. She looked genuinely distraught.

'It's awful good of you to come. I'm going to miss Paschal. I know we couldn't live together but he was a decent skin and not the worst by far.'

This seemed to be high praise in her vocabulary. Paul invited Finn to come along with family and close friends to the pub across the road from Milltown Cemetery to have a drink and a sandwich. Finn declined. He did not really know Paschal's family and he was in no mood to sit drinking with a lot of old people reminiscing. He'd been to too many funerals over the years and could not face another one.

He caught a black taxi outside the cemetery and rode down to the bottom of the Falls Road. He walked from there to Kelly's Cellars. Despite it being a rainy Tuesday afternoon, it was pretty full. Some of those sitting at tables or standing at the counter seemed to be habitués. Others looked like shoppers sheltering from the rain. Finn ordered a pint of Guinness, not his usual but he knew it was Paschal's preferred tipple. He watched as the barman went through the venerable ritual of pouring the pint. Finn let the stout settle in the glass before he picked it up.

'Here's to you, Paschal. May you rest in peace.'

XVII

Finn's Testimony

I T WAS THE TENTH ANNIVERSARY of the Good Friday Agreement. The newspapers, radio and television were full of features marking the occasion. Finn viewed all this with increasing anger. There were so many programmes that featured the widows of RUC men, or wounded British soldiers, or victims of IRA bombs. 'What about us?' he found himself asking the television after one such programme.

My uncle Christy was an ordinary man. A husband, father, brother, son, and uncle. He was married with four children. He left school at fourteen and trained to be a heating engineer, and by the time of his death he had his own business. His partner was a Protestant and they employed Catholics and Protestants with no thought about anybody's religion. Christy was a family man who kept in close touch with his parents and brothers and sisters. He gave employment to any of his nephews who wanted it. Like my own parents, he moved from the Loney on the Falls Road to a three-storey house off the Cliftonville Road in North Belfast. They were among the first Catholics to move into this area, but were not the last.

In February 1977 a car drove into his street after dark. It was a UVF gang who came to this street because they believed only Catholics lived there. Doors were closed and blinds drawn everywhere except for Christy's house. Eileen, his wife, was out with friends and he was at home babysitting. He left the front door open and the lights on for her coming home. That was how they picked his house. The men who killed him rang the doorbell and fired blindly through the frosted glass of the inner door when Christy came out to answer it.

Only one bullet hit him, but one was enough. He died hours later in hospital after doctors had removed the bullet from his brain and tried to save his life.

I will never forget taking the phone call that night to say he was shot, nor seeing my mother collapse onto a sofa in shock when I told her. I still feel the trauma of having to phone his brother in England and tell him. Then do the same thing hours later when word came through that Christy had died. I was just nineteen at the time.

Christy was loved by everyone who knew him. He was no saint; he had his faults, and may have fallen out with people from time to time; but he was a good decent man. He was tall, with movie star good looks, and a quiet but imposing way about him. He knew how to have a good time and, when coaxed enough by one or other of his sisters, he occasionally sang at parties. He did not play much with us as children but he had something about him that made us admire him. When he spoke to you, you knew he took you seriously and he always had an encouraging word for me. When I started university, he gave me a lift across town every morning as it was on his way to work. I got to know him better then, as an adult, not just someone I looked up to as a child. We never discussed what was happening around us. He was too wrapped up in his family and his work to worry about politics. He would listen while I talked of university life and what courses I was doing.

I remember seeing men, hard men, who were his brothers-in-law and friends, cry at his funeral. I can never forget the wails of his wife and sisters as the coffin was taken from the house, and perhaps worst of all the silent grief of his mother, my granny, unable to take it all in.

My uncle Christy never wore a uniform, never sent men out to kill or be killed. He was not an Earl or a member of Cabinet. Decades later, no one rushes to the microphone to condemn his murder. He was just a Catholic from North Belfast. No one wants to make a documentary about the day he died. No one calls for a memorial in his memory, or demands an apology for an innocent life taken. My uncle Christy is just a statistic.

Since that night I always make sure to lock the front door of our house after dark. I never leave a light on in the hallway.

I never go to sleep without the thought that a phone call will wake me up with terrible news. I don't live in North Belfast anymore. I live miles away in every sense from the Troubles, but that makes no difference.

Christy was not the only one. Two years later two men called to the home of my uncle Jimmy. He and his wife, Alice, were out in a nearby street visiting friends. The gunmen sat for an hour and a half in the sitting room with their daughter who was only twelve years old. When Jimmy and Alice came home they shot him dead in front of his child and wife. Alice ran after them as they escaped and they shot at her too. Luckily she was uninjured.

My friend, Aidan, whom I'd known since primary school was a decent man, the proverbial gentle giant. He had a wife and family, and had no interest whatever in politics. He was in the Fire Brigade and like many firemen had a part-time job to fill in the time on his days off. He drove a taxi for a Catholic firm. One night he was called to pick up a fare at the Chichester Park Hotel. The men who got into the back of his cab shot him in the head four times, leaving him for dead. He managed to crawl out of the cab and along the carpark to the steps of the hotel. An ambulance took him to the hospital but he died shortly after. Just a fortnight before, he risked his own life to save that of a man trapped by a fire on the Protestant Shankill Road. There were many more like him.

The memorials for most of these dead are the headstones over their graves. They get barely a mention in the TV programmes, books, and articles produced about the Troubles. No one interviews their survivors and says what a shame it is that a twelve-year-old girl saw her father shot dead in front of her. We hear of British Army and RUC widows and orphans, but scarcely a word about the widows and orphans of those innocent Catholic men shot down, or kidnapped and tortured to death. There is a hierarchy of victims in the Troubles and we, the Catholics of North Belfast, are on the bottom rung.

The Author

ANTHONY CANAVAN grew up in North Belfast during the Troubles, in which he lost both family members and friends through violence. He attended St Malachy's College before going on to Queen's University Belfast, where he studied history and politics. After graduating from QUB, he began his career as the Curator of Newry Museum in County Down. While there, he wrote *Frontier Town, an illustrated history of Newry*, which was shortlisted for an Irish Book Award in 1990.

On his marriage in 1996, he moved to Dublin, where he began work as a freelance editor and reviewer before joining *Books Ireland* magazine. He is currently Consultant Editor with *Books Ireland*, after serving as the magazine's editor for a number of years. He is also a regular contributor to *History Ireland* magazine, and over the years he has written articles for academic books and other publications on history, culture, film, and literature.

POVERTY IN IRELAND 1837
A Hungarian's View — Szegénység Irlandban
by Baron József EÖTVÖS   216 pages, 70 illustrations, bilingual

ISBNS (HBK): 9781908420206   (PBK): 9781908420213

IRELAND BEFORE THE FAMINE

'An extraordinarily lucid and "modern" account of the desperate conditions and suffering that prevailed in Ireland in the decade preceding the Great Famine...'
—*DUBLIN REVIEW OF BOOKS*

'The Tragedy of the Irish – through Hungarian eyes ...Should be among the recommended readings for the responsible citizens of the European Union...'
—*CENTRAL EUROPEAN POLITICAL SCIENCE REVIEW*

'One of the Best Irish Books of 2017 – The first thing the book does is demolish the fiction that Irish people were well-fed before the Famine. Ten years before it started they were already half starving in the streets...'
—*IRISH CENTRAL, NEW YORK*

'...acutely accurate...a vivid and gripping tale...totally contradicts the official story of Ireland peddled by its then administrators.'
—*BOOKS IRELAND MAGAZINE*

'Baron József Eötvös was horrified by what he witnessed'—*HISTORY IRELAND*
'A wonderful text...a fascinating insight'—*HUNGARIAN CULTURAL STUDIES, PA.*

CONFIDENT FRENCH from A to Z
—A Dictionary of Niceties and Pitfalls
by Michaël ABECASSIS   208 pages,   125 illustrations

ISBN (PBK): 9781908420183

'...This is a lucid, informative and hugely entertaining book of French grammar and usage. ...a concise and illuminating explanation of all aspects of the language – ranging from general grammatical points to idiosyncratic usage of words and phrases, from pronunciation to orthography... This indexed and alphabetically-ordered book, abundant in quotations from authors and examples from everyday French, could be utilised by anyone studying French, but will appeal most to those with intermediate ability or above. It is a delightful book, with numerous illustrations by Igor Bratusek, visualising the content and thus facilitating its internalisation by the reader. **This work should be heralded as a major contribution to the pedagogy of French in our times.'**
—*GENGO NO SEKAI JOURNAL,* TOKYO [*'THE WORLD OF LANGUAGE JOURNAL'*]

"Lovers of French will enjoy the latest book by Dr Michaël Abecassis"
—*WADHAM COLLEGE NEWS,* UNIVERSITY OF OXFORD

"An amusing but serious guide to the vagaries of French from a lecturer at the University of Oxford"—*BOOKS IRELAND MAGAZINE,* DUBLIN

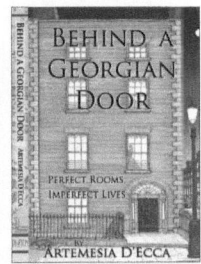